Ante's
INFERNO

GRISELDA HEPPEL

Ante's
INFERNO

Wood engraving for cover by Hilary Paynter
Cover design by Pete Lawrence

Matador
9 Priory Business Park,
Wistow Road, Kibworth Beauchamp,
Leicestershire. LE8 0RX
Tel: (+44) 116 279 2299
Fax: (+44) 116 279 2277
Email: books@troubador.co.uk
Web: www.troubador.co.uk/matador

Wood engraving for cover by Hilary Paynter
Cover design by Pete Lawrence

ISBN 978 1780882 406 (SB)
978 1780882 413 (HB)

British Library Cataloguing in Publication Data.
A catalogue record for this book is available from the British Library.

Typeset in 12pt Aldine401 BT Roman by Troubador Publishing Ltd, Leicester, UK
Printed and bound in the UK by TJ International, Padstow, Cornwall

Matador is an imprint of Troubador Publishing Ltd

For
Rebecca, Léonie, John and Michael

CHAPTER ONE

Solo

The grass was wet underfoot. It soaked through Ante's shoes, chilling her feet till they felt as numb as her fingers, curled around the cold metal trumpet. Wriggling her toes, she fought the impulse to jump up and down. Not a good idea when the breeze was already blowing her black hair in wild, frizzy strands across her face and flapping the hem of her skirt against her knees – her *knees*! How many other girls had hems that long? Very few, judging by the groups making their way across the football pitch towards her, interspersed by knots of boys in their grey trousers or shorts.

She grimaced. The uniform had felt wrong from the start, grey pleats and long woollen socks doing nothing either for her solid build or her dark skin. Now it felt even worse as the whole of Northwell School gathered in a semi-circle before her, staring...

She shook herself. *Don't be stupid.* People were looking at her because of where she stood, that was all. OK, so some of the younger ones might be whispering and giggling but it wasn't directed at her.

It wasn't *them*. Glancing around, she felt a flicker of hope rise in her chest. They weren't even there. They must have decided to bunk off. *Yes!* One thing less to worry about.

A stillness settled on the crowd. Gusts of wind shook raindrops from trees nearby and tugged at red poppies, loosely tucked into button holes. All eyes turned to the headmaster, standing on the other side of the tall stone cross from her, about to begin.

Not all. A movement, there, on the left… *no*. Not them, it couldn't be. They should be hiding out in the changing rooms, too cool for this whole Remembrance thing. Not here, calmly threading their way to the front, the others shrinking back to let them through. Ante forced her gaze upwards, above their heads, above everyone, trying to focus on the jumble of roofs and tall chimneys that marked the school buildings in the distance. Anything not to see what was now straight in front of her.

There was no point. The figures were etched on her brain. With her eyes closed she could have picked out Florence's delicate features, the wave of blonde hair across her forehead; then Shelley's shining braids, smooth against her perfect black skin; and finally Alex's pale, pinched face and sharp green eyes. She could even have predicted Alex choosing the moment the Head began to speak to turn to Florence and mouth those horrible words, making Florence crease up with laughter.

Pain shot through her fingers as they tightened round the trumpet. That name again! If Alex had chanted 'Ante E-le-phantee, Ante E-le-phantee!' out loud it couldn't have rung in her ears more than it did now, as she stood like a great clumsy idiot, waiting to sound her trunk, oops, no, *very* funny, her trumpet – while they waited for her to mess it up.

Don't look at them. Don't look at them and everything will be OK. She fixed her attention on the Head's stern profile, letting his words swirl in her mind before being lost to the wind. 'First World War…tragic slaughter in the trenches…many old pupils from this school, some barely out of their teens…terrible hardship, as those of you in Year Seven are learning in History…' History! She'd forgotten her homework on trench warfare, Mr Matthews would go *crazy*… Her gaze wandered away to encounter – *them.* They were still staring at her. Three pairs of eyes, blue, brown and green, stared into hers, above smiles playing over pursed lips.

'John Hawkins, Edward Horrocks, David Lonsdale…' The names of the fallen blended into one solemn, continuous murmuring. *Please, please, let the list go on. On and on forever. Then I don't have to play.* But at last the Head ceased; a brief echo from the crowd, and away in the distance a church clock struck eleven.

Silence. A steady hum of traffic drifted across from the far side of the school buildings. Ante moistened her lips and breathed softly down the mouthpiece, making no sound.

Then Mr Randall caught her eye and she raised the trumpet. All fidgeting in the crowd ceased. People stood still, head bowed and hands by their sides, until the final notes of the *Last Post* faded on the air.

★ ★ ★

'Well done, Antonia – I mean, Ante. I'm sure your father would've been proud of you.' Mr Randall strode through the crowd making its way back to the classrooms, his eager eyes sending wrinkles all the way up his large forehead, over which grey wisps of hair floated in the wind.

Pride swelled in her chest. 'Really?'

For that alone it was worth it. The practice, the nerves, the loneliness – not just standing there on her own, but from the beginning of term, joining the school for the last two years instead of in Year Four like everyone else. Her dad would've stood at the back, head on one side, not looking at her, not wanting to break her concentration; then at the end there'd be a quick, warm smile from his eyes, a wave and he'd be gone.

'Definitely. Keep it up and you'll be the one with your own jazz band one day.'

'Thanks, Mr Randall!'

'Next thing we'll have you playing in is the Christmas concert. Let's see now – I've got a music class in the assembly hall first lesson this afternoon. Come by just before – ten to two, say, and we'll talk about it.'

She gazed after him, aching to burst into a grin, her insides in turmoil. That rush of feeling, like when the letter first arrived – months ago now – with the news she'd won the music scholarship, when her mother had squealed and hugged her and they'd both danced round the room, that same sensation surged through her again. She was *good*. She could do this! Northwell School with its odd traditions and uniforms, its cluster of ancient, turreted buildings, parkland and playing fields rolling down to the river – so different from the crumbling concrete and brick walls of St Dunstan's – the whole place might still feel strange but things would work out. Surely, once she got used to her being there, even Florence would –

'*Thanks, Mr Randall.* Quite the performer, aren't we?'

Her chest tightened.

Florence came nearer. 'You just have to be the star, don't you, Ante? You and no one else.'

How could hissing sound so gentle? She shrank away but immediately straightened; Shelley and Alex had positioned themselves uncomfortably close on her other side.

'Standing up there, all eyes on you, I bet you think you're *really* something.'

Heat swept up Ante's throat. 'I – I don't, I just – look, I didn't ask to do that. It was Mr Randall. He – made me.'

'Oh, come on, Ante, we're not at St Dunstan's anymore. You can stop pretending.'

Ante stopped dead at the edge of the playground. 'What do you mean? Pretending what?'

'No one can make you do something, Ante Alganesh. It's your choice. Like when you chose to – ' Florence broke off, biting her lip.

Ante stared at her. 'Chose to what?'

But Florence shook her head and set off across the playground so fast that Shelley and Alex had to run to keep up.

'Chose to WHAT?' Ante didn't care if people were staring; what was this all about? 'St Dunstan's? Florence, you left after the first term!'

The doors to the classroom block swung shut. Ante stared at the empty space. '*That* term,' she murmured.

December, six years ago. Frost in rivulets on the pavement and sparkling on car windscreens. Light catching her mother's hair and separating it into strands of spun copper as she bent to zip up Ante's anorak before swivelling round to wave goodbye. And Ante, dazzled by bright metal of wheels and handlebars, screwing up her eyes to catch her father's last smile as he set off, ear flaps of his ridiculous sheepskin cap lifting in the wind, down the road that took him away forever.

CHAPTER TWO

Breaking Point

Oh hell, they'd waited for her.

If staying on after History to explain about her missing homework had made Ante late for lunch, at least it should have meant she could eat it in peace. Florence, always at the front of the queue, should be finished and gone by now; not sitting round a table right by the food counter, Shelley and Alex beside her and a few other classmates who'd be perfectly nice if Florence wasn't there.

Clutching her tray, she focussed on the grey-flecked lino under her feet. Not on the sniggering and exchanged glances and – worse – the silence that fell as she approached. A silence broken by the slight, fair-haired figure in the middle who began to hum, beating time gracefully with her slim hand as Ante's still-soggy feet clumped closer.

'Ah, Ante. There you are.'

Ante's heart thumped in her chest. *Take no notice.* No way was she going to sit with them. She could go somewhere else, sit by herself like the other loners.

Slowly, she walked past the table.

But Florence's words seemed to wrap themselves around her legs and pull her back. 'Ante, perhaps *you* can help. You're the musical one.'

No. Don't stop. Don't turn round.

'Naa-na-naa-na-naa-naa,' sang Florence, as if to herself. 'No, I can't work it out. Which do you reckon works better? "*Ante* E-le-*phan*tee" or "An*toni*a E-le-phan-*toni*a?" The second one's a bit clunky but – '

Something rushed through her. She couldn't hold it. Her tray crashed down on the table between Florence and Shelley. Water from the glass splashed her hand but she felt nothing. All she could feel was the bright blue eyes laughing up at her as she leaned over, speechless, gripping the tray so hard her finger nails cut into the wood.

'Woah, temper, temper. Isn't it time you learnt to control that?'

Faces around the table seemed to dissolve. Dimly from the right came Shelley's voice, trying to intervene. 'Florence –'

All was drowned as her own voice tore through her, scraping her throat and bursting out in a cry that wouldn't stop. 'I hate you, Florence, I hate you, I *hate you!*'

She shot out her hand and grabbed the nearest thing within reach: a pepper pot. Her arm jerked through the air and suddenly the blue eyes were no longer laughing. Florence fell back in her chair, face screwed up, sneezing and coughing.

'You *c-cow*, Ante,' she choked, 'I'll get you for this!'

Ante's hand fell to her side. She felt limp suddenly, exhausted.

What had she done? The pepper…Florence's eyes…no! She hadn't been as close as that, hadn't meant –

'Out of the way!' An elbow hit her in the ribs as Shelley lunged forwards holding a glass. Bodies crowded round, blocking Ante's view of the water hitting its target so that all she could hear was spluttering and gasping and at last, Shelley's soothing tone: 'It's OK, Florence, you'll be OK. It's not that bad.'

A wave of hope rose in Ante's chest. Through a gap in the shoulders turned towards her she glimpsed pale features dappled with red blotches, eyes blinking… *blinking.* Florence must be all right then, surely she wouldn't be able to do that if –

A flick of lank hair. From the other side of the table Alex's sharp chin raised in her direction. '*Get her*,' she hissed. 'We're going to the Head *right now.*'

Faces spun round, mouths set hard. Hands seized her arms. No, not the Head, not that! Twisting away from the fingernails digging into her flesh she wrenched herself free, scarcely noticing the stabs of pain, and ran from the dining room. Along the passage, through the door to the outside, cold air striking her face – damn! The pepper pot was still in her hand. Stuffing it into her pocket, she shot down the steps and into the playground. She had no idea where she was going, all that mattered now was to get away. Fast.

A clunk behind her as the door swung shut, muffling

the sound of feet thundering in the corridor, the cries of outrage – they were all after her! She dashed across the playground towards the main school building, scattering marbles and getting in the way of football games as she went. People yelled but she didn't stop. Up the steps, into the lobby – here at last she paused, breathing hard.

Dark panelling covered all four walls. Straight ahead wide polished wooden stairs led upwards. To her left, glints of aluminium and glass marked school photographs hanging either side of the door into the assembly hall; to her right lay the corridor along the science labs. If she slipped down this she could emerge at the other end and – no! Of course the door would be locked during lunch, why didn't she think of that? Stairs then, but which way? Down to the changing rooms, gloomy, hidden away, ideal if you wanted to corner someone – or risk the floor above, only containing staff room and store cupboards and out of bounds to pupils?

No time to think. Heart beating hard, she shot up the forbidden staircase, reaching the landing just as the main door banged open and feet charged through, racing down the stairs to the changing rooms. Pressing her hot palms against the wall, Ante leaned back and closed her eyes. They would never dare come up here. She was safe.

Familiar voices emerged back up the changing-room stairs, arguing angrily.

'Well, I don't know, do I? It was Florence who reckoned she'd be in the dungeons, not me.'

'She must've gone into the hall instead.'

'Yeah, well, she won't be in there now, it's no use looking. I said we should check there first.'

'Why didn't you then? If you thought it was such a brilliant idea…'

The main door closed and the voices ceased. Ante remained where she was, trying to gather her thoughts.

She was in deep trouble. That was certain. Her first term not yet over and she'd done something so awful as to send her straight to the Head. To the Head! What would he do? An answer shot into her mind and her knees turned to water.

Not that. Please, please, not that. She clenched her fingers so tightly the nails cut into her palms. She'd do anything, take any punishment, if only he'd give her another chance, prove the scholarship hadn't been a mistake, she could handle herself…

Handle herself. That was a joke.

It wasn't as if it had been an equal fight. Hadn't she just attacked a girl half her size and strength? What did that make her? Supposing – a new thought struck her with a force that made her reel – supposing she really *had* hurt Florence, *had* damaged her eyesight? It didn't look like it; but what if Florence had collapsed just afterwards, that even now she was being rushed to hospital… Ante's blood ran cold.

Then she remembered. *It was Florence who reckoned*

she'd be in the dungeons, not me. Someone in that state wouldn't be up to reckoning anything. Nor would Shelley and Alex have abandoned their friend to chase after her. She began to breathe more easily.

Click. Her heart jumped. The main door opened again and someone with light footsteps walked to the bottom of the stairs. Too light for a teacher. Someone who knew exactly what she was looking for and where to find it.

'Ante. I can tell you're up there. It's no use hiding, you know. Not after what you've done. You might as well come down now and save me the trouble.'

She pressed herself back against the wall, gripping the wooden panelling to stop herself shaking. *Keep calm. She's bluffing. She won't really come up here.*

'Fine. If that's the way you want it.' The stairs creaked.

Ante looked around her. No escape. The oak-panelled wall rose straight ahead. To the right, the corridor that led to the staffroom: it might be empty, all the teachers being at lunch, but she couldn't be sure. Suddenly her eye fell on a door she hadn't seen before, cut into the panelling at her side. Seizing the handle, she slipped through, closing the door behind her.

For a minute she couldn't think where she was. Gradually shapes and lengths of darkness sharpened into the outlines of a wooden balcony sticking out half-way up a huge room, no, a hall... of course. The assembly hall, the oldest part of the school, dating back hundreds of years apparently, long before Dr Northwell arrived on the scene. And this must be the organ loft, now used only to hold the lights for school plays and concerts.

Her body tensed. She was no safer than before; Florence could find the door any second. Deeper into the gloom, that was her only hope...*ouch*. Those damn lights! She grabbed at the balcony rail for support and – *it moved under her hand.*

Shrinking back, she scrabbled behind her for the wall. The blood beat in her ears as she flattened herself against the plaster. That had been a close one. Best keep away from the rail.

'Ante.' A crack of light appeared. 'You're in here, aren't you? Come on, Ante, I know you are.'

Don't move. Don't even breathe.

The crack of light grew. 'Congratulations, scholarship girl. You just got yourself expelled.'

Against the brightness of the landing the blonde head wore a halo of gold. Ante bit her lip, feeling the skin tighten under her teeth.

'Did you really think you could attack me and get away with it?' Stepping forwards, Florence peered into the darkness. 'Thought you could barge into Northwell School and have everything your own way, just like at St Dunstan's?'

Sweat trickled down Ante's neck. In the blackness behind her eyelids, she seemed to see Florence lunge at her, nails aiming for her face. Wincing, Ante struck the back of her head on the wall.

'Because I have news for you.' The voice became sweeter than ever. 'Things have changed since we were little. You got away with it then. Not anymore.'

Florence's hand was on the rail. Ante inhaled sharply.

'*There* you are,' Florence cried. 'Think I can't see you?'

She walked forwards. Ante, trembling, watched the hand move along the rail. *I should warn her*. She opened her mouth but no sound came out.

'Scared of me, are you?' jeered Florence. The rail moved slightly but she didn't notice. 'You should be,' she added softly, letting her hand bear more weight as her feet squeezed past a spotlight.

Ante gasped. *I must warn her!* But it was as if her throat had closed and she couldn't breathe, couldn't form the words, and the image flashed across her mind of this hand creeping towards her freezing suddenly, of something happening to prevent –

Crack. A tremor seemed to go through Florence. The smile vanished from her face. And in that moment Ante saw what she hadn't seen before.

They were not alone. Next to Florence, intense, grey eyes gazing straight into Ante's, stood the dim, shadowy figure of a boy. No time to think who he was or how he'd got there.

'Get back from the hand rail,' she cried, her voice suddenly free. 'It's not safe!'

The next moment came a crash and a scream and the sound of old, dry wood breaking into splinters. For a split second Florence's face, white as death, seemed suspended in the air; then something hit the floor below with a sickening thud.

Dizziness swept through Ante. Her legs gave way. She fell against the wall but the wall itself seemed to be sliding away from her, sending her toppling backwards. A shape rushed past her, followed by a hard edge scraping the length of her shin, like the bottom of a door swinging back into place – then all was darkness.

CHAPTER THREE

Gil

Stunned, Ante lay where she had fallen.

Something terrible had happened. The hand rail had given way and Florence…no. That horrible thud, that couldn't have been her, it *couldn't…*

But the total silence all around bore its own clear, inescapable message. *If Florence was safe she'd be here too, here in this darkness – and so would the strange boy…*

Wait. This darkness. How could it be dark? She must be in shock. Or maybe unconscious. In a moment she'd come round and all would be clear. She forced herself to breathe calmly, to allow her whirling thoughts to subside and the darkness to clear from her eyes.

It didn't. It was real then. Yet it couldn't be. She'd fallen against another exit from the organ loft; she should be back in the bright electric light of the landing, with the corridor to the staffroom straight ahead.

But there was no light. It was cold, with a strange dampness in the air and a smell of earth and stone. The floor under her bruised body felt hard and uneven, nothing like the linoleum of the school corridors, nor the splintery floorboards of the old organ loft. Instead she seemed to be in some sort of tunnel, a pale glow in the distance suggesting that it came out somewhere – but where?

'What the hell – Ante?'

She nearly cried out with relief. A shaft of dim light and there stood Florence, silhouetted against the opening. Ante would have leapt to her feet and thrown her arms around her, yes, around her worst enemy – if the enemy hadn't been shaking with outrage and fury.

'You're not getting away from me, Ante. Just you wait!'

Her relief evaporated. She pressed herself against the wall of the tunnel, hard bits of rock digging into her ribs. *It's dark. She can't see me.*

'Ante?' Florence's voice wobbled. Her outline shifted as she stepped into the gloom. 'Where are you?'

Ante held her breath. Footsteps fell within centimetres of her, passing her, heading down the tunnel. *Go on. Just a bit further, enough to let me slip back through the door...*

An idea came to her. Softly, very softly, she felt on the ground for a loose stone and hurled it towards the pale light in the distance. With a crack the stone hit the side of the tunnel and carried on, ricocheting down.

Florence gave a cry. 'Got you, Ante! You won't get far, whatever you're up to down there.'

Now's my chance. Rising to her feet, she turned to the door.

It wasn't there.

She felt all around the tunnel wall. Her hands slipped off the gritty surface, the rock here sticking out, there disappearing into hollows, but nowhere revealing the slightest opening. The door had disappeared.

She stared into the darkness. There had to be an answer to this, there *had* to, if she could only keep calm and think it through.

'It's no use. There's no going back. I've checked.'

She wheeled round.

'I'm here.'

Only blackness. Nothing and nobody to be seen.

'Come on, Ante,' the voice continued, moving gradually away from her. 'We'll have to go through the tunnel. It's the only way out.'

'Who are you?' Ante whispered, following. 'How do you know my name?'

'I was in the organ loft with you, remember? Rather hard *not* to know your name, the way Madam there was throwing it around. Didn't notice you doing much talking, though.'

'No, well, I was trying to hide from her. Hey, wait for me!'

'Hurry up, then.'

Ante quickened her step.

'She seemed really upset about something, that friend of yours,' said the boy, after a few moments' stumbling along together in the dark. 'Nearly knocked me over, shooting past like that.'

'She's not my friend! I hate her!'

'Whoa, calm down, no need to bite my head off, girl.'

Ante swallowed. Stupid, hysterical female, this boy must be thinking, they work themselves into a state about nothing at all. She drew herself up. 'We just don't get on very well, that's all,' she said, with what she hoped was a dignified air.

'I could see that.'

The darkness began to thin. Turning towards the boy, she was just in time to see him snatch his gaze from her and focus determinedly on the ground. Puzzled, she regarded his profile. In the loft she'd glimpsed a shadowy, almost ghost-like figure; yet there was nothing shadowy about the solid, stocky boy now walking beside her. They were roughly the same height and he seemed about her age – so why didn't she recognise him from school? He was wearing a very odd kind of uniform: instead of the normal navy blue sweatshirt and grey trousers, he had on a battered-looking grey flannel jacket and shorts that came down to the knee, long, thick woollen socks and scuffed black lace-up shoes. She brought her gaze back to his face only to see him look sharply away again, as if afraid to catch her eye, yet unable to stop staring. What was *wrong* with him?

'Who are you?' she asked. 'And why do you keep looking at me like that? Stop!'

The boy obeyed. They weren't far from the mouth of the tunnel now and the light was stronger. A pair of startled grey eyes looked into hers from under a mop of thick, tousled hair, whose sandy colour was matched by the generous sprinkling of freckles over his nose. The effect was oddly cheerful, even though he wasn't smiling.

'Well? What are you looking at?' she repeated.

The boy blinked. 'Sorry,' he muttered. 'It's just – well – I've never seen anybody black before.'

'What? Do you go around with your eyes shut all day then?'

'No – I – er – ' He reddened under her sceptical gaze and looked away. But the next moment his eyes shot to her face again and a note of excitement entered his voice. 'Are you from Africa?'

'No.' Ante smiled. How stupid was this boy? 'But my dad was. From Ethiopia. He came over here to be a doctor.'

'Oh.' The boy nodded, eyes still large and round.

She tried again. 'So, who are you? What's your name?'

'Gil.'

'*Gil*? What kind of a name is that?'

'Same kind as yours, I imagine.'

Now it was Ante's turn to blush. 'Sorry. You're right, I've got an unusual name too. It's short for Antonia, which I don't like very much. What's yours short for? Gilbert?'

'No.' He spoke sharply. 'It's not short for anything. I'm just Gil, all right?'

'Sure,' said Ante, puzzled. 'But who are you? Why've

I never seen you before? Which class are you in?'

'Hold on!' cried Gil. 'What's this, an interrogation? I don't know why you've never seen me before, any more than why you should suddenly see me today. I'm in – well, I *was* in Upper 4B. I'm thirteen,' he sighed, as Ante looked at him blankly.

'Year Eight, then. I'm in Year Seven. But – but – ' Ante frowned. She thought she knew everyone in the top two years by now, at least by sight. And his class – upper four something – what was that about?

'Look.' His gaze slid away. 'I can't explain all this. I don't understand it myself. All I can tell you is that I've been on that organ loft quite a long time.'

'What, were you hiding, too?'

'No – not exactly. I was sort of – trapped.'

'Someone chased you in there!' Ante couldn't believe her luck. Here at last was an ally. 'So you know what it's like to have people pick on you,' she rushed on, 'who won't leave you alone, who go on and on at you until you can't bear it any longer and – '

'Yes, yes.' His eyes darted round the walls. 'Shouldn't we carry on and see where this tunnel comes out? That might make things clearer.'

That told her. She'd only just met this boy and here she was, jabbering away – would she never learn when to keep quiet? She was still mentally kicking herself when they reached the mouth of the tunnel.

Then every thought went clean out of her head.

CHAPTER FOUR

The Styx

'What on earth – ?'

A rocky hillside rolled away from her, with a path that wove down between low bushes and plants to the bank of a wide, dark, marshy river, on which stood a wooden jetty.

Ante spun round. The mouth of the tunnel gaped, its jagged edge obscured in places by overhanging tufts of grass. Above, the hillside continued upwards to meet a wide, grey sky.

Heart beating wildly, she retraced a few steps and peered into the darkness. Nothing. *Keep calm,* she told herself. *It's not real, none of it.* She closed her eyes, turned to face forwards again, counted to three and tore them open.

It was all still there. Bushes, rocks, footpath, jetty – silvery grey against dank, stagnant water – if it was water and not a mass of oozing slime… But where was the school? Her breathing quickened and she hurled herself up the slope behind, grappling for handholds in the dry earth.

'Where are you going?' A couple of metres below Gil looked up at her.

She stared at him. Sweat plastered a lock of hair to her forehead and she wiped it away. 'Back, of course. I don't know where we are or how we got here, but school must be somewhere and if we don't – hey, watch it!'

'Sorry,' he panted, letting go her arm and leaning back on the slope. 'But I told you. We can't go back.'

'What?' The wrist taking her weight buckled and she sat up, clutching it. 'What do you mean, we can't go back? Where are we, anyway?'

She looked around. Below lay the river, its far side swathed in a heavy, rolling mist. On either side of them the hillside stretched away, seeming to curve in towards the river in the distance; it looked almost as if, beyond the mist, the curves might join together, like the rim of a giant green bowl. Trees grew here and there and some way to the left began to cluster into a large forest. But that was all. Not a single house or road. Not even a wall, fence, gate or track. No sign of any kind of human habitation.

'Gil, what is going on here? For god's sake, tell me where we are.'

'I – I'm not sure.'

She gaped at him. His forehead creased slightly, as if he felt they'd just taken a wrong turning somehow. *A wrong turning* – what, from halfway up the assembly hall in the middle of Northwell School?

'What do you mean,' she cried, 'you're *not sure*?'

He hardly seemed to hear her. 'This must be right, though,' he murmured. 'All those people…'

She followed his gaze and saw that theirs was not the only path down the hillside.

Some distance away, a small group made its way towards the river. They seemed mostly elderly and in their best clothes: the men in dark suits, the women in flowery or plain-coloured dresses. A party of senior citizens on an outing? But there were younger ones too: a girl in a pink strappy top and jeans with a multi-chained belt; a big man with sunglasses, dressed from head to toe in motorbike leathers, even a couple of children in football shirts. Beyond this strange mixture of walkers there must have been more paths, because other groups were scattered over the hillside, those furthest away like tiny, multi-coloured specks, all moving steadily in the same direction.

'Who are all these people?' she said. 'And where are they going?'

The second question, at least, she found she could answer herself. They were clearly all heading for the jetty, already dotted with figures. But as they drew near, most people didn't turn left on to it; instead they carried on, following a path that gradually sloped upwards, until the river fell away below them and they vanished into a soft, bright mist; a mist that couldn't have been more different from the grim, dark cloud that rolled over the river.

Bewildered, she turned to Gil again. 'Gil, please, do

you have any idea where we are? Or what we do now?'

He shrugged. 'This is it, I suppose. The green mountain. We're here at last.'

'The green – *what are you talking about?*'

Ante stared at him. His pale eyes gazed solemnly into the distance. There was a tinge of uncertainty, disappointment even, in his expression; but he didn't look raving mad. *It's a dream. I must be dreaming. Soon all this will melt together and disappear and I'll be back at school.*

'It's odd though,' said Gil, his frown deepening. 'It doesn't look right, somehow. The mountain should be rising above us, high into blue sky. Not sloping down to a river. Er…Ante – why are you looking at me like that?'

'I'm waiting for you to disappear. And me to wake up. It's the only explanation.'

'You think this is all a dream?' he smiled. 'No. I know dreams. They're over now.' Sighing, he started down the hill.

Ante didn't move.

'Come on, Ante, let's join the others. We might find your friend then.'

'My fr – ? Oh, Florence!'

She couldn't believe that Florence had slipped her mind for so long.

'How many times do I have to tell you, Gil,' she panted, running to catch up with him, 'that Florence is not my friend? You heard what she was like in the organ loft.'

'She was certainly going on at you about something,' he conceded. 'What did you do?'

Ante hesitated. *I half-blinded her because she was calling me names* didn't sound good. 'Nothing. She just hates me.'

He raised his eyebrows but to her relief didn't pursue the matter. There was no more time to talk anyway as they'd reached the river and plunged into the crowd streaming along the bank. Ante found herself next to a thin, pale young woman with fine cheekbones, whose forehead under her silk scarf showed smooth and much too high.

'What happened to your hair?' she blurted out.

'It'll grow back.' The woman smiled down at her.

'Hey, does that go for me too, do you think?' said a balding middle-aged man in a smart suit and tie.

'Not a chance, curly,' came from behind.

Ante looked round for the speaker and spotted him among a group of soldiers in camouflage striding along; not marching, not carrying weapons, but laughing and joking with the rest. Further away, more people in other kinds of uniform and styles of dress dotted the line: flowing white cotton robes and saris, brightly printed pareos and plain black head scarves; some people wore heavy overcoats and fur hats as if they expected deep snow and ice. She jumped aside just in time to avoid a small child in shorts and t-shirt darting through the crowd.

'Sorry,' he giggled before leaping forward and

touching a girl with long, shining black plaits. 'You're it!'

'This is the weirdest crowd I've ever seen,' Ante whispered to Gil. 'Where can they all be – oh!'

A tall black man with tightly curled, slightly receding hair had just looked at her with a quick smile. The years fell away and she was a little girl again, sipping lemonade and jiggling up and down in the vast, dimly lit community centre, letting the jazz flow through her, waiting for the moment when the band leader would finally lower his trumpet and give her a wink.

'What is it Ante?' said Gil. 'Are you all right?'

She swallowed. 'Yeah. That – that guy. He reminded me of my dad. Which is crazy.'

'Why?'

'Because my dad's dead.'

Gil shrugged. 'That's not crazy. He could be further on. Hey, something's happening up there.'

Ante's mouth fell open. Didn't Gil understand anything? 'I told you, he's dead! Killed by a lorry on his way to work, nearly six years ago. Just before Christmas.'

Now he turned and looked at her. 'I'm sorry Ante. That must have been tough.'

'It was. So – what did you mean, he could be further on?'

But they had drawn level with the jetty now and Gil was absorbed by the sight of three young men in tight black jeans and baseball caps who held clipboards on which they ticked off the people as they passed. Each wore a t-shirt, also black, but emblazoned with a huge design of golden crossed keys; and slung across his shoulders, a large pouch, bulging with shining gold coins.

'Look at them!' hissed Gil in her ear. 'Have you ever seen such stupid hats before? Why would you want the brim at the back and a hole at the front?'

Ante didn't reply. With difficulty she turned her mind to what the clipboard men were doing. Each person handed them something before being ticked off and sent on the upward path into the bright, silvery mist. No one turned left on to the jetty.

'They're ticket collectors,' she said. 'But I don't have any money.'

'Don't be silly, of course you do.'

She stared at him. 'No, I haven't,' she repeated. 'Why do you say that?'

'Check your pockets. There'll be a coin somewhere. Look, this is mine.'

He drew out a dark, well-worn coin with uneven edges, about the size of a ten penny piece. From over Ante's shoulder came a sharp intake of breath; it was the woman with the headscarf again but this time she wasn't smiling. Her face wore an expression Ante couldn't quite read: a mixture of surprise, disappointment and, yes, disgust.

Nor was she the only one. On all sides people shrank away, leaving their path clear to the men with the clipboards. Ante glanced round, eyes darting from face to face. No one returned her gaze. She stiffened as muttered questions rippled through the crowd like a chill breeze. 'See that?…What can they have done?… So young, too…'

'Name?' The inspector looked at Gil, pen at the ready.

'Gil Marow.'

'Gil…Gil…Gil…' He scanned his clipboard. 'That short for anything?'

'No.'

'Hmm. Funny, I can't seem to find – wait a minute.' He flicked swiftly through the pages. Then he gave a low whistle. 'Not short for anything, eh? Who's this then? Virgil Marow. Reckon that's got to be you, don't you?'

Gil stared down at the ground.

'*Virgil?* Oh Gil, is that really your name?' Ante couldn't stifle a snort of laughter.

Gil glared at her, his cheeks crimson.

'Took your time, didn't you, Virgil?' said the inspector. 'Come on then, hand over your coin.'

'It wasn't my fault,' mumbled Gil as he held it out. 'I tried to come before but – '

'What?' cried Ante. 'You tried to come *before*?'

Her eyes flew to his face, searching for a clue that would make sense of all this; but he seemed to have forgotten she was even there. 'What's the matter?' he whispered.

The inspector stood immobile, transfixed by the sight of the solid, dark coin in Gil's hand. 'Not this way for you, my lad. Only gold coins go round the Styx. You have to cross it.' He pointed past Gil's shoulder to the jetty.

'The Styx?' cried Gil. 'That's the *Styx*? But – that *can't* be right! I thought – '

He wheeled round, blocking the jetty from Ante's view. Beyond him, pools of black, oily water spread between clumps of withered marsh grasses until all was lost in grey fog. She shuddered.

Turning back, he gazed at the line of people climbing into the shining mist above him, as if, by will power alone, he could somehow reach through and join them.

'It is for you,' said the inspector. 'No good looking at the other path. So, come on – '

'Wait,' cried Ante. 'What's going on? What d'you mean, Gil, you tried to come before? Where *are* we, anyway?'

The ticket inspector broke in. 'I'm sorry, young lady, but you'll just have to wait your turn like everyone else.' He turned to Gil. 'Off you go now.'

Gil looked at Ante. Something new mingled with the bewilderment in his eye – was it fear? Turning, he walked down to the river without a backward glance. The crowd parted to let him through.

On the jetty stood about a dozen men and women of different ages; some leaning against the railings, some sitting on the edge, blank eyes gazing into black water.

Some wore balaclavas or headscarves that covered all their features; others might just as well have done, by the total lack of expression on their faces. Nobody was smiling. And there were no children.

Ante rounded on the inspector. 'You can't make him go with those people!' she cried. 'He's just a boy on his own, he – '

'Look, I don't know who you are, but you can't tell me what to do because it's my job, see? Now you've wasted enough of my time already. Name?'

She didn't reply. Out of the fog on the river loomed a large, dark shape. Nearer, it solidified into the rusty hull of a boat, steered by a massive, crouching figure. Black, oily gobbets of water slid down the punt pole in its hand and splashed on to the wooden bench at its feet.

'It's the Boss,' said one of the other ticket inspectors. 'Quick, get this line moving or we'll be in for it!'

'For the last time,' Ante's inspector was saying, '*what is your name?*'

'Ante,' she said hurriedly. 'Ante Alganesh. Who – who's that?'

The boat bumped the jetty. The crouching figure rose and became a huge, hairy man in a filthy robe, who climbed out and stood sizing up his passengers. One by one he ordered them into the boat with a jerk of his chin and they followed dully, as if all life had been drained out of them long ago. Ante strained to see past the ticket inspector, now flicking distractedly through sheaves of paper on his clipboard, to keep the jetty in view. The ferryman had not yet reached Gil.

'I can't understand it,' moaned the inspector. 'Your name isn't anywhere here.'

'Never mind that.' Ante's eyes darted back to his. 'I haven't got one of those coins either, gold or dark. Just tell me what's going on down there. That boatman – where's he taking them?'

The inspector dropped his clipboard and, to Ante's amazement, buried his face in his hands. 'Not another one,' he groaned.

'What do you mean? Not another what?'

But then she saw, out of the corner of her eye, that the jetty was nearly empty and the last person – Gil – was about to get on to the boat.

Giving the ticket inspector a shove that sent him reeling into the arms of his colleagues, she shot through the crowd. 'Wait!'

Gil halted. The boatman wheeled round, eyes blazing, hair and beard streaming behind him. 'Who dares set herself against the will of Fate?' he thundered.

Ante quailed. What was this, some kind of madman?

'Show me your coin!'

'I – I haven't got one.'

'Haven't got one? Fabian!'

The ticket inspector scuttled down to the jetty.

'How many more of these stowaways have you got for me today, hmm?'

Fabian looked very pale. 'No more, sir, I hope, I don't know what's going on today, I – '

'So.' The boatman gazed at Ante, one gnarled hand still grasping the pole, the other combing through his long matted beard. His eye fell on Gil who had edged back to join her. 'I suppose you're with this female?'

'Yes, he is,' said Ante.

'And the other one?'

The *other* – ? Oh. Florence. *That* other one. 'Yes,' she sighed, after a brief hesitation. 'We're all together.'

'Then go. Off, the pair of you, and find your friend. Fabian will show you what to do.'

Hitching his dirty cloak over his shoulder, he stepped down among his sullen cargo and pushed away from the jetty. In seconds the boat with its dismal contents vanished into the thick, dank mist.

CHAPTER FIVE

Finding Florence

'Right.' Fabian straightened up. 'Here's how it goes. If you come here without a coin, for whatever reason, you need a return ticket to get you home once you've crossed the Styx. Traditionally, this has been in the shape of a golden twig, or bough. You should find one in that wood over there.' He pointed to the hillside behind them, where the grassy slopes gradually gave way to low scrubland and then to clusters of trees that formed the forest. 'That's where I sent your friend. Looks like she hasn't found it yet. Of course, she may have run into – '

'Look,' said Ante, wearily, 'I don't want a return ticket. I don't want to go anywhere in this place except home.' *And I'd like to go there now, please. It can't go on much longer, this dream.*

Fabian stared at her. 'But you can't go home. Don't you realise where you are?'

'No!' She almost screamed with exasperation. 'Everyone here seems to know what's going on except me! Why doesn't someone just *tell* me where we are?'

Fabian and Gil exchanged looks.

'Hades,' said Gil. 'We're in the land of Hades, Ante.'

This should mean something to her – his solemn tone said so – but what? She waited a moment. Then, 'What's Haydees?' she said.

This time they both stared at her in total amazement. Gil's large grey eyes became even larger and rounder.

'What? *You don't know what Hades is*? What have you been *doing* in all your Latin and Greek lessons? It's the only interesting bit there is.'

'We don't do Latin and Greek,' replied Ante. 'They're dead languages.'

'I know *that*. But it never stopped us having to learn them.'

'Look,' broke in Fabian, 'I'd really like to stay and chat but I have work to do.'

'*Chat?*' Ante cried.

But he was already halfway up the river bank. Reaching his post, he stopped and turned round, shouting something back at them, lost in the chatter of the crowd.

Gil frowned. 'What did he say?'

'"Watch out for the circus," it sounded like,' said Ante. 'Whatever.'

For a moment Gil looked baffled. Then he shrugged. 'Oh well, never mind. Come on, I'll explain things as we go along.'

They left the jetty and crossed the line of people on the bank, turning right towards the forest, against the flow of the crowd. Some glanced curiously at them as they passed, but no one spoke and gradually the people diminished in number as the little tributary paths thinned out. Soon they were stumbling alone over the uneven, tussocky ground.

'Hades,' said Gil, 'is the Underworld. Or it's the name of the King of the Underworld, I forget which. The ancient Greeks and Romans believed that when they died their spirits came to the banks of the Styx, waiting for Charon to ferry them across. Each soul had a coin which they gave to Charon to pay for – '

'Now, just a minute,' interrupted Ante. 'Are you saying we're in an Underworld dreamt up by a bunch of people who died thousands of years ago? That's ridiculous.'

Gil nodded. 'I know. I didn't understand it myself at first. I knew I was meant to go somewhere but I never thought it would be like this.' He paused. 'Ante, I've got to tell you something. When you saw me in the organ loft, back there, can you guess how long I'd been stuck in it?'

'Don't know. Since break, maybe? This morning?'

He shook his head.

'Since *yesterday*? *Longer*? But hasn't anyone missed you?'

'September 1910.'

'But that's – that's a hundred years ago…' Her voice trailed away. Something cold and shivery ran down her spine. She sank into the grass, finding it strangely difficult to breathe.

'Is it?' Gil sat down next to her. 'Well then, 25ᵗʰ September, a hundred years ago, was the day of my death.'

'The day of your – *death*?'

This solid, clear-eyed boy, his socks wrinkled down to his scuffed shoes, with red patches on the backs of his knees where the rough cloth of his shorts had chafed, this wasn't flesh and blood, this was a *dead* person? A – a *ghost*? But ghosts were dim and shadowy, transparent even…

Shadowy. Like Gil had been in the organ loft. On the other side of the door that disappeared. She bit her lips. 'How – how did you die?'

'I fell off the organ loft. Or rather, I was ki – I mean, pushed.'

'You were *pushed*?'

'Yes. By – another boy. He made me sit on the rail. Then he pushed me off. I hit the floor headfirst.'

The rail. Florence's hand on the rail. Ante felt something clutch at her stomach.

'Why?' she brought out at last. Her mouth felt dry.

'Because I'd – ' he stopped and stared down at the ground.

Ante waited, not daring to speak while, mouth set hard, Gil tugged savagely at tufts of grass and flung them away from him.

'Because you'd – ?'

He shot her a glance, seemed about to say something, then looked away again. 'He hated me,' he said at last, shrugging his shoulders.

'What?' Ante sat up straight. 'Enough to kill – *murder* – you? But how – why?'

A flush stole up Gil's neck, spreading over the pale, freckled skin. His mouth twisted. 'I dunno.'

Ante felt a surge of anger. Just what kind of a place can Northwell School have been? Beside her Gil sat with his head bent, blinking, chapped lips in a tight line, his hands gripping his crossed ankles so that the tips of his fingers showed white against the crumpled grey socks. Biting the inside of her cheek, she forced her voice to keep steady. 'So what happened to him?'

'Nothing much, I don't think. When they found my body he was blubbing all over me, swearing it was an accident, we'd been fooling about.'

'You mean he got *away* with it?' Ante leant forwards so far she nearly lost her balance. 'That's unbeliev– ' She broke off. Falling back, she sat for a moment utterly still, aware of nothing but her own breathing.

An accident. Like with her and Florence. It could be Florence lying there while she…

Strands of hair trembled before her face as she stared downwards. *No. That was different, completely different.* Straightening her back with effort, she focussed her mind on Gil's story. 'But someone must have seen it all, surely?'

'Not in the middle of the night.'

'The middle of the – you mean, you *slept* there? Northwell used to be a boarding school?'

'Of course.' He looked surprised. 'Don't you? Oh. I

thought maybe they'd turned one of the boys dormitories over to girls – either that, or added a fourth.'

'A fourth – you mean there were only three for the whole school? It must have been tiny!'

'Not that tiny.' He looked slightly put out. 'There were nineteen of us when I started. Twenty-three by the time my brother arrived. I suppose it's grown since then.'

'It has a bit.' Her mind grappled to piece it all together. 'Then – are you saying you've been haunting the organ loft for the last hundred years? Why has no one ever seen you?'

'I don't know. It was like – have you ever had that dream where you're somewhere crowded, a railway station, or – or a park or somewhere, and the people are all doing things and chatting together and you want to join in but it's as if someone has switched off the sound? As if you're watching through glass and no one knows you're there?'

Ante nodded.

'It was like that. I saw Dr Northwell entering the hall every morning, my school fellows getting out their hymnbooks, Mrs Northwell appearing next to me, her fingers on the organ keys – all in a kind of dreamy silence. After a while I suppose I fell into a dream myself.' He paused for a few moments, head bowed, a lock of sandy hair falling across his forehead, his fingers playing with a stem of grass. 'But I knew, all the time, that I didn't belong, that somewhere, something was calling me, pulling me away from the organ loft. I'd close my eyes and I'd see this green mountain rising high into a clear blue sky, with a path winding up and up till it disappeared out of sight – then I'd open them and be back where I was.

'And then' – he jerked his head up – 'one day, out of the blue, *you're* there and first thing I know, I'm hearing again. The creak of the floorboard, the other girl arriving and giving you a piece of her mind, then the crack of the hand rail and the tremendous crash – it was a shock after all that silence, I can tell you. But nothing like the shock I got when the door appeared and you fell through it.'

They looked at each other.

'So I've been wondering,' said Gil at last, 'why now? Where do you come in all this? Why do you have the power to open a door that's been closed to me ever since I died?'

Ante shook her head dumbly. She had no idea.

'And there's another thing that's been bothering me,' said Gil. 'The hand rail.'

Ante's heart lurched.

'What took you so long? You knew it was broken. I was *willing* you to warn her but you left it till the last minute. Any longer and she could've fallen into the hall and cracked her head open, like I did. In fact at one point I thought – ' He broke off, reddening slightly, and scrambled to his feet.

Ante didn't move. She stared downwards, feeling

herself grow hotter and hotter. *Thought what? What?*

But Gil just stretched out his hand. 'Come on. Hadn't we better go and find her?'

Ante took his hand and stood up. She couldn't return his smile. *He must never find out. Why I didn't – couldn't – he must never guess the truth. If he does he'll never speak to me again.* Her cheeks burned and she avoided catching Gil's eye.

Gil didn't appear to notice. 'Then I suppose we'll have to find this wretched golden – hey, what was that?'

A scream, a sudden, high-pitched scream of pure terror hit their ears like a thunderbolt. For a split second they stared at one another; then, from the direction of the forest, the cry came again, this time mingled with something far worse. A tearing, snarling sound.

'It's Florence!' cried Ante. 'Something horrible has got her – quick, Gil!'

But he was already racing for the forest. She followed, running and stumbling over the rough ground.

CHAPTER SIX

Two's Company...

From behind a clump of trees a huge, black, spiky shape lunged towards them.

'Gil!' screamed Ante. '*Gil*!'

Snarling drowned her cry. Teeth flashed and sank into Gil's sleeve; he yelled and struck out but other jaws snapped at his head, his body and his legs and suddenly all Ante could see was a blur of limbs and fur, claws and teeth and dust. Her eye darted around for something, a stick, a stone, anything that could serve as a weapon. Plunging her hands into her pockets, her fingers closed on a cold, hard shape. The pepper pot! She tore it out and shook it at the snapping teeth with all her might.

The jaws exploded into racking coughs and sneezes and fell back. Gil, scratched and bleeding, dragged himself out from under the choking pack of dogs, or rather pack of dog...

'Gil,' cried Ante, 'it's got *three heads*!'

'I know,' he panted. 'Come on.' Grabbing her hand, and half-limping, half-running, he led her to something lying pale and motionless only a few metres away.

It was Florence. She lay on her back, eyes closed, hands resting near her head, the sleeves of her sweatshirt torn and dirty, a long red scratch running down her cheek.

Ante felt cold inside. 'Is she – is she all right?' she whispered.

Gil nodded. 'Just fainted, I think. We'll have to bring her round fast. Cerberus won't be out of action long.'

'Ser – what did you call it?' She looked behind her.

Choking had given way to whimpering as the creature lay stretched out, eyes still streaming, taking it in turns to rest one of its three shaggy heads between its front paws, clearly not being able to make up its mind – minds – which one needed most care.

Gil bent over Florence and shook her by the shoulder, first gently, then with increasing urgency. At last her eyes flickered, opened and looked straight into his. He stood perfectly still. His lips parted to say something but nothing came out.

Oh no, thought Ante. *Oh no, no, no.*

'Who are you?' Florence gazed up at Gil in bewilderment. Then she caught sight of Ante. 'Ante, you're here too! What's going on? What is this place?'

If she hadn't known better, Ante could have sworn Florence was pleased to see her. A strange feeling, somewhere between surprise and hopefulness, stirred within her. 'Are you OK?' she said.

Florence sat up. 'I – I think so.' Pushing strands of

hair behind her ears she glanced round. 'Something horrible attacked me – oh!' She shrank back again, her eyes wide.

Ante spun round. Black, slavering lips bared three sets of white teeth. A low, deep growling emerged from the throats as the shaggy creature lumbered to its feet.

Gil started. 'Quick!' Reaching Florence a hand to help her up, he set off at a run towards the forest.

Ante launched herself after them. Brambles snagging her sweatshirt and tree roots catching her ankles she ran for several minutes until at last, aching and out of breath, she grabbed at a tree to stop herself. For a second branches, leaves, glimpses of white sky and straggling undergrowth whirled around her head. Then all was still.

'It's OK,' she panted. 'It's not following us.' With a sigh she collapsed on to the thick, silvery grey root of an ancient beech tree sticking out of the sandy hillside. Not the most comfortable of seats but better than nothing.

Gil threw himself down nearby while Florence, a short distance away, leant back against a tree trunk and closed her eyes. For a moment, no one spoke.

'Right, Ante,' said Florence. 'Tell me where we are and what's going on.'

Ante saw the expression in those steely blue eyes and the brief stirring of hope left her. Business as usual, then. She braced herself. 'I don't understand it any more than you do. I – I know this sounds crazy, but according to Gil here' – she glanced at Gil, sitting between them – 'we're in some weird place called Hades, or the Underworld, or something, and it's – it's the place you go when you die – '

'*What*?' Florence sat straight up against the tree trunk. 'Ante, you can't be serious. Are you trying to tell me we're – we're *dead*?'

'I don't think so – ' Ante began and stopped. Florence's face rose before her, deathly pale against the gloom of the organ loft, her body lost in darkness. Clasping her arms round her knees, she stared downwards, blinking hard.

'You don't *think* – ?'

Ante gave herself a shake. Florence had to be all right, she just had to be. 'I – well, we'd know if we were, wouldn't we? For certain, I mean. Like Gil does.'

She nodded towards Gil, who was tugging out small pieces of beech root from the soil next to him and trying hard not to look at Florence.

'Like – *Gil*?' Florence's voice fell to a whisper. She turned slowly to look at him, as if afraid of what she might see.

Gil carried on jabbing at the ground, his fingers solid, a pink flush spreading up his neck. Nothing shadowy about him. Florence's brow creased in puzzlement.

'Go on, Gil,' prompted Ante, 'tell her your story. You could start with your name at least. Actually, we should be calling you Jill, not Gil, as it's short for Virgil – oh, except people might think you were a girl. I mean, they wouldn't really,' she added hastily, as he swung round to glare at her.

'Ante,' said Florence, 'that's not very nice of you. You shouldn't make fun of people's names.'

'I wasn't ma – '

'You've got a really interesting name,' Florence smiled at Gil. 'I like it. Where does it come from?'

Ante was speechless. *I'm not the one who makes fun of names, you are!*

But Gil gazed at Florence with gratitude and frank admiration. 'My father was nuts about Classics,' he explained, turning his back on Ante completely. 'I think he hoped I would be too, but I'm not much good at Latin and Greek and all that. He called me after his favourite Roman poet who wrote some long, long poem about the fellow who founded Rome, I can't remember who. He didn't think about all the teasing I'd get, but I can tell you, I hated my name the minute I started school. I shortened it at once.'

Florence nodded. 'It must be awful to be teased like that over something you can't help.'

Ante felt she was going to explode. *Yes it is! You know how awful it is because you're an expert at it!* She buried her face in her arms and bit her lip until it hurt. How could she have made such a mess of things? Her own clumsiness had allowed Florence to turn the tables on her; Gil would never believe her side of the story now. All she could do was listen as Gil, suddenly fluent under the warmth of Florence's sympathy, poured out his tale.

'Let me get this straight,' said Florence when he'd finished. 'You're saying you've been trapped in the organ loft for a *hundred years*? That's unbelievable!'

Gil nodded and gave a slight shrug.

'Until today when Ante, of all people,' Florence's voice was sugary sweet, 'opens a door that releases you into the Underworld. But – why?'

'No idea.' Ante shifted in her seat as the blue eyes rested on her, their expression hardening.

'And here's a problem,' Florence continued. 'It's not just Gil who goes through, but you and me too. So now we're trapped on the other side. Well, thanks a bunch, Ante. Nice mess you've got us into.'

'What do you mean, I've got us into?' Ante flared up. 'I didn't know the door was there, did I? If you hadn't chased me into the organ loft – '

'You were the one running, not me. You'd lost it completely. I was worried about you, that's why I followed.'

Ante gaped at her. She looked at Gil. Surely he wouldn't swallow this one. But he avoided her gaze. Scooping up some dry, sandy soil, he poured it from one hand to the other.

'And then what happens?' Florence went on. 'I get practically torn to pieces by this horrible, snarling monster – and would have been, too, if you hadn't saved me!' She turned to Gil, her eyes glowing.

This was too much for Ante. 'He didn't save you – I

did. I – I threw pepper in its face. Faces. I couldn't think what else to do.'

Her voice trailed away. Oh, why hadn't she kept quiet and let Gil take the credit?

But he stared at her in amazement. 'That was you! And I thought it was just an incredible stroke of luck, Cerberus getting a sneezing fit! Quick thinking, Ante.'

He grinned at her. Suddenly she felt warm again.

'Well, well, well, it's back to the old pepper trick,' cut in Florence. 'Getting quite a dab hand at that, aren't we, Ante? Funny how you always seem to have a full supply of pepper with you. I suppose you never know when you might bump into a three-headed dog.'

Heat rushed up Ante's neck, burning her cheeks. Gil looked from Florence to Ante, clearly puzzled.

'Go on, Gil,' said Florence, 'ask her why she happened to have a pepper pot on her. Just at the right moment.'

As he hesitated, Ante seized her chance. 'Look,' she said, jumping to her feet, 'hadn't we better get a move on? We have to find this return ticket – this golden bough – to be sure of getting home. That's what the guy said.'

She could feel Florence glaring at her back as she led the way towards a path running through the trees. *So let her! As if she cared!* Stiffening her neck, she began to search all round as she walked. Green and yellow leaves dappled across her vision until they mingled into one shimmering mass, unbroken by even the faintest gleam of gold. Her head began to ache.

'Oh, I'm fed up with this,' groaned Florence. 'How are we supposed to find – '

'Ssh.' Gil stopped. 'Listen.'

From somewhere in the trees ahead came a soft, cooing sound.

'It's only a bird,' said Florence. 'So what?'

'Haven't you noticed?' replied Gil. 'It's the first we've heard. Don't you think that's strange? Woods like these should be alive with birds.'

'Perhaps not in the Underworld,' said Ante.

'It's a wood-pigeon, I think,' said Gil, 'or maybe a turtle dove.' Overtaking Ante, he plunged down the path.

Moments later his cry came back. 'Hey, come and see!'

CHAPTER SEVEN

The Golden Bough

In a small clearing stood a tall, dark tree composed of several stems of different thicknesses, rather than a single trunk. Its leaves were like holly, only longer and thinner, the prickles not so sharp. Perched on a branch near the top, a white turtle dove regarded them with something like satisfaction in its beady eye.

All this Ante noticed fleetingly, for what really drew her was a glimmer among the dark green leaves near the bottom of the tree. A single shoot of pure gold, about as long as her forearm, grew out of the ground, surrounded by much larger, woody stems.

Beside her, she heard Florence's sharp intake of breath. Gil, too, stood gazing in awe.

'There's something written on the bark.' Florence pointed to the thickest of the trunks that made up the tree. 'It looks like a poem.'

Ante bent closer. In small, clear, gold lettering, the ends of the lines running a little way round the trunk so she had to keep moving from side to side to read them, was written:

You who walk the rings of death
While yet your body draws its breath,
Take the bough that glitters here;
Protection will it give from fear
And bring you, when your journey's done,
To look again upon the sun.
But if you steal to make your gain,
Nothing can it bring but pain.
Yours is the crimson stream that runs
And calls for aid the kindly ones.

'Oh, great,' muttered Florence. 'We can *take* the bough but not *steal* it. What's the difference?'

'I don't understand,' said Ante. 'If we steal it, it'll bring us pain, but then somebody kind will turn up and help us, so where's the problem? What do you think, Gil?'

Gil wrinkled his brow. 'I don't know. There's something that bothers me about this, something I ought to know. But I can't think what it is.'

'We have to take the bough anyway, it's our return ticket,' said Florence.

'Right, here goes then.' Grasping the stem, Gil gave it a tug.

A fearful, ear-splitting shriek tore through the air. Ante clapped her hands over her ears and shrank back. Hunching his shoulders, Gil tried again.

'Stop!' Ante grabbed his arm. 'It's screaming at you, Gil!'

He snatched his hand away as another shriek, higher than the first, drowned her words and pierced her brain. Staggering, Ante fell back down the path, Gil and Florence stumbling behind her. Once out of sight of the tree, she paused and risked a look back.

Silence.

Dropping her hands from her ears she let out a long breath.

'*Now* what do we do?' sighed Florence.

Gil stood, hands on hips, head bent, a bead of sweat trickling down his brow. 'I think,' he panted, 'you and Ante have to do this alone. You're the ones who need the return ticket, not me. I – I shouldn't have touched it.' His eyes flicked from Florence to Ante and back down on the ground.

Ante nodded. A note in his voice seemed to catch at the back of her throat and she looked away.

'OK Ante,' said Florence, 'it's down to us then. Come on.'

Us. Yeah, right, thought Ante. She followed her back up the path and watched, muscles tensed, hands ready to cover her ears, as Florence reached out.

A breeze rustled the leaves above. That was all. Ante let her arms sink back to her sides. With a little cry of satisfaction, Florence closed her fingers around the stem and pulled. And pulled again. Slipping her hand to the base of the shoot, she tried to bend and break it off.

No good. The bough remained rooted in the ground.

'Let me have a go,' said Ante.

Florence shrugged and sat back on her heels. 'If you like.'

Bending forward, Ante grasped the bough. Instantly a tingling feeling flowed up her arm and through her body. From the roots of her hair to the soles of her feet, she felt bathed in a warm, golden glow.

Beside her came a gasp. 'How did you do that?'

Ante looked down at her hand. Gold against her dark brown skin, the bough nestled in her palm, bearing no trace of broken stem or root. It was as if it had slid into her fingers the moment they touched it. 'I – I don't know.'

'Give it here.' Florence stood up.

That warmth, that sense of wholeness – no. She couldn't bear to part with it. Not just yet.

Florence smiled at her. 'Just for a moment, Ante. I only want to see what it feels like.'

The bough was in Florence's hand before Ante realised what was happening.

'Oh,' Florence breathed. 'It's beautiful.'

'Isn't it?' said Ante. 'I'd like it back now, please.'

Florence didn't seem to hear her. She was concentrating on sticking the bough into the belt of her skirt.

'Hey, what are you doing? It's mine!'

'No, it's ours.' Florence looked up. 'And I'll look after it. You'd only lose it and then we'd all be in trouble.'

'Who says I'd lose it?' cried Ante. *I'm* the one who picked it, not you. Give it back!' She made a grab for the bough but Florence caught her hand in both of hers and forced it away.

'Listen to me,' said Florence. 'Fair's fair. You ended up getting the bough, but I must already have loosened it.'

'What?'

'You know, like breaking the seal on a jam jar. It came to you far too easily, you have to admit.'

Ante's hand fell slowly back to her side. Was that how it happened? It kind of made sense.

Florence smoothed down her skirt. 'So,' she said, 'we did it together. And what does it matter who carries it? It's for both of us, after all.'

'But – ' began Ante. Florence sounded so reasonable, it was hard to object. And yet…

'Oh come on, Ante.' Florence rolled her eyes. 'Tell you what. We'll ask Gil what he thinks. Which of us should look after it, I mean.'

That did it. Not hard to guess which of them Gil would support. Ante groaned.

'Good. I'm glad you've seen sense.' With a last check that the bough was in place, Florence started down the path.

Ante followed, teeth clenched. Whatever the argument, it didn't feel right. She'd plucked the bough, not Florence. It was hers! Blinking, she rounded a group of trees just as Gil leapt to his feet, his freckled face lit up with a smile.

'Florence, you've got it!' he cried. 'Well done.' Then his eyes fell on Ante. 'What's the matter with you?'

'Nothing.' She stared down at the ground.

'Yes there is. You look as if everything's gone wrong when in fact it's all gone right. Florence has the bough. You're both safe now, don't you understand? You can get back.'

Rawness rose in the back of her throat. She nodded, her mouth shut tight.

'Actually, Gil, I'm afraid that is the problem,' put in Florence. 'I'm the one with the bough. We picked it together, you see. But Ante wanted it for herself.'

'Oh for goodness' sake, Ante,' cried Gil. 'What does it matter who's got it? It's for both of you, isn't it? You don't half make a fuss about things, you know.'

He started down the path, shaking his head in disbelief, Florence walking swiftly beside him.

Ante let them go ahead a few paces. Then she followed, jaw clamped to keep back the tears.

★ ★ ★

'You never warned us about the guard dog,' said Florence, when they'd reached the jetty. 'What's it doing there?'

'Yes,' added Gil. 'I thought Cerberus sat in a cave, guarding the way. Not leaping out of the woods at people.'

The boatman raised a thick, straggly eyebrow. 'You had your warning from Fabian,' he said. 'If you chose to ignore him, that is your affair.'

Gil opened his mouth to protest. Ante glanced at him

nervously but he closed it again without speaking. Behind the massive figure glaring down at them, the rusty boat lay still on the dark water.

'My passengers show no great willingness to come with me,' growled Charon, motioning them into the boat. 'What use is Cerberus chained up in a cave if they flee to hide in the forest? Imagining' – he snorted, swinging himself on board after them – 'that thus they might escape their fate.'

The sneer in his voice sent a shiver through Ante. She huddled on her bench behind Gil, while above her the boatman thrust his pole against the jetty, sending them gliding into the gloom.

'But that's what I don't understand,' said Florence, her back to the bows. 'If your passengers want to escape, you must be taking us to some horrible place which all those people over there' – she nodded at the stream of people mounting cheerfully into the bright mist above the receding bank – 'don't have to go to. So why does Gil?'

No reply. Staring into the darkness, Charon pushed the punt pole down and pulled it up again, splashing Ante with evil-smelling water as he did so. Each time he bent his ancient knees, his joints creaked alarmingly, as if his legs might snap.

After a few minutes, he stood up straight and still. A long, dark shoreline loomed through the mist towards them, sending the boat into even deeper shadow.

'Well, why?' pursued Florence.

The coals in the boatman's eyes blazed. 'It is not for you to ask questions, nor for me to answer!' he roared. 'I follow Fate, I do not order it! For your friend it is ordained that he must travel the circles of Hades until he reaches his destination. I do not know what terrible thing he has done to deserve this, nor what task he must do, nor why he has you for companions; still less do I care. Rise now and go!'

Coldness settled on Ante's shoulders and ran down her spine. She gripped the edge of her seat with both hands as the boat bumped the soft, oozing shallows. Through the mist a mass of tree roots curled into the water, like fingers waiting to wrap themselves around her legs as she stepped out...

Don't step out. The thought shot into her mind from nowhere. *Make the boatman take you back. You don't even have to be here, only Gil.*

Only Gil. Sitting with his back to her, motionless, fists clenched by his sides so that the knuckles showed white. Closing her eyes, she let her head fall back as a shudder darted through her body. *No.* She'd taken this on and she couldn't back out now. If Gil must go, she would too. And Florence...

In the bows a pale face stood out against the gloom, eyes wide, mouth set firm, one hand clutching the ray of gold at her belt. Ante sighed.

Florence was part of the package.

CHAPTER EIGHT

Elysium

Stagnant air coiled around them, heavy with the smell of decay. Holding her breath, Ante dug her fingers into the bank while mud sucked at her feet and tree roots caught at her ankles. Nearby, a beam of light danced where Florence pulled herself up, her outline sharpened by a tall black, jagged shape yawning through the mist above them.

Ante's heart lurched. Gritting her teeth, she heaved her body up to stand beside Florence and Gil. Pale rock now appeared to the right of the blackness, revealing it to be the mouth of a cavern, deep within which metal glinted. A chain fixed to the wall trailed across the floor, beside it – *ugh* – a scattering of half-gnawed bones.

'Cerberus's cave,' said Gil, peering in. 'At least we know it's empty.'

Standing back, Ante ran her eyes along the rock wall beyond the gaping mouth, where a path followed round the crag, disappearing to the left as the ground fell away. In the distance, dark mountains formed the horizon. She seemed to be on the brink of a gorge so immense that the far side was almost invisible. Hollowness opened at the pit of her stomach.

'Florence – Ante – look!' cried Gil.

Ante spun round and caught her breath. On the other side of the path, a meadow rolled away to a line of trees, grey-green against a golden sky. Poppies, cornflowers and wild garlic waved in the long grass; stepping forwards, she closed her eyes and breathed in deeply. A scent of honey filled the air.

'No prizes for guessing which way we're meant to go,' muttered Gil, glumly turning his back on the meadow.

'Who says? I know where I'd rather be.' Kicking off her shoes, Florence plunged into the soft turf, shoes in hand.

That was enough for Gil. With a whoop he ran after Florence and Ante followed, feeling the breeze rush through her hair, cool and fresh after the dank and slimy waters of the Styx. Reaching the line of trees she threw herself down in the shade beside the others, laughing at the soft tickling of grass on her skin. Maybe this journey wasn't going to be so bad after all.

'Silence!'

Gil and Florence froze. Ante sat up straight, pulling grasses and flowers out of her mouth and hair, and looked round. The command had come from nowhere. Scrambling to her feet while Florence fumbled with her shoes, she couldn't repress a cry of astonishment.

Before her lay another stretch of grassland, not wild

like the meadow, but flat, green and completely smooth, like a cricket pitch. Which was what it was, for there at one end stood a man wielding a bat while a woman in a long, strangely-draped dress prepared to bowl. Other men and women were dotted around the pitch in fielding positions, wearing, not the usual cricket whites, but different coloured tunics, belted around the waist and ending just above the knee. Most spectacular of all were the helmets worn by the two batsmen and wicket-keeper: shining bronze, they came down in a long V-shape over the face, with almond slits for the eyes and crowned with a Mohican-style plume. Their shin-pads, too, were of bronze, finely following the shape of their lower legs; in fact they weren't shin pads at all, of course, but –

'Greaves! They're wearing armour!' cried Gil at her shoulder.

'This is *bizarre* – ' began Florence.

'Silence, I say!'

A short way away, on the gentle slope that led towards the pitch, stood a tall woman in a long white tunic fastened at both shoulders by elegant brooches. Her hair was piled high on her forehead in tight, black curls with some pulled back to form an elaborate arrangement at the back of her head. She was watching the game intently.

Thwack! A great shout went up and Ante's eyes flew to the pitch. Metal flashed as the batsmen's faces swivelled in their direction. The first player threw down his bat and strode towards them; or rather, towards the figure on their left throwing the ball in the air and catching it again, her dark eyes sparkling with triumph.

'*Cass*,' he groaned, 'I might have guessed. Can't you ever let a fellow get a century?'

'I told you,' replied the lady, 'you will get your century. The day after tomorrow, just before tea. And not a minute sooner.'

'I don't know why you bother playing when you always know what's going to happen.' Flinging himself down on the grass, he pulled off his helmet and ran his fingers through his hair; dark, Ante noticed, and surprisingly long. Halfway into the action, he stopped. 'Hallo there! What's this, Cass? You never told us we'd be having visitors.'

The lady sighed. 'You know very well there would be absolutely no point if I did. But now I will introduce you. Hector, these are Virgil, Antonia and Florence.'

Ante gaped.

'I am Cassandra, daughter of King Priam of Troy,' continued the lady. 'This is my brother, Hector.'

Florence was the first to recover. 'How can you possibly know our names?'

'Ah, that's my sister for you,' laughed Hector. 'She can see the future. Not that she bothers to keep us informed much,' he added, giving his sister a side-long glance.

Cassandra pursed her lips.

61

Hector jumped to his feet. 'Come and have some refreshment and tell me about yourselves,' he said, walking the three of them down towards the pitch. 'You especially,' he cried to Gil, 'I have longed to meet. You captured the cruel deception and fall of Troy so truthfully in your poem – '

'Er – ' stammered Gil.

'Not *the* Virgil,' said Cassandra coldly. 'He was only named after him.'

'Oh.' Hector turned away.

Gil looked slightly crushed, as if for once he longed to live up to his name rather than be rid of it. They crossed the pitch in an awkward silence, making for a group of trees with a table underneath. Drawing nearer, Ante saw that it was covered with delicious things: peaches, grapes and strawberries, fresh bread and honey, olives, figs and jugs of wine. She'd had no idea how hungry she was.

'Odysseus, we have visitors. Virgil, Florence and Antonia.'

'Welcome, friends.' A powerfully-built man, with a brown, weather-beaten face and laughter lines crinkling the corners of his eyes, bowed and waved his hand over the table. 'Eat your fill. Guests in Elysium are rare enough.'

'Thank you,' murmured Ante, taking a strawberry and allowing it to burst in her mouth, rolling its warmth and sweetness on her tongue. Next to her, Hector broke off a handful of fresh, crusty bread, dipped it in honey and handed it to Florence. Only Gil remained completely still, open-mouthed and wide-eyed.

'Elysium – the Elysian fields!' he managed at last. 'Where all the heroes go when they die.'

'True, my young friend.' Odysseus smiled, handing him a large, ripe peach. 'Look around you. We're all here.'

He nodded to where Cassandra had joined the other players scattered about the grass, some sitting, some lying full-length, eyes closed, helmets and greaves discarded nearby. Ante let her eyes wander towards a figure in a long, pale blue robe, sitting a few metres away in the shade of some trees. Beside her stood a strange-looking object resembling a large wooden clothes horse, with about twenty stones hanging from it on lengths of string.

'Looks like Aeneas is playing court to your wife,' said Hector, giving Odysseus a sideways grin as the other batsman, a tall, broad-shouldered man with close-cropped hair, strolled towards the lady, a goblet of wine in each hand.

'Ha. Is he, now?' Odysseus raised one eyebrow. Draining his cup, he plonked it down and stretched out his hands to the three of them. 'Come, friends. We will join them.'

CHAPTER NINE

Penelope's Gift

Taking the goblet offered her, the lady looked round and smiled. Close to, the strange contraption by her seat solidified into a hand loom, the weighted strings holding a piece of cloth woven with a complicated and beautiful pattern.

'Florence, Virgil and Antonia,' said Odysseus, 'this is my wife, Penelope. Oh, and this,' he added, nodding at the other batsman, 'is Aeneas.'

Gil could hardly contain his delight. 'Aeneas, I remember now!' he cried. *'You're* the one Virgil wrote about, the great hero who escaped the Sack of Troy and founded the Roman Empire.'

The man bowed. As he straightened up, his eye chanced on Florence and stayed fixed. 'It is many ages since one entered Hades bearing what you bear,' he said.

A lock of blonde hair fell forward as Florence looked down at herself. 'Oh, the bough. It's my return ticket. Mine and hers, that is,' she added, gesturing at Ante.

Ante ground her teeth. *Thanks, Florence. Kind of you to remember me.*

'So,' said Aeneas, 'you are here to discover your progeny, the generations of illustrious descendants destined to spring from your womb – '

'*What?*'

'While Aeneas was still alive he, like you, paid a visit to Hades,' explained Odysseus. 'And he also had – what did you call it? – a return ticket to protect him. To very few mortals is given this power. For Aeneas, it was so that he could meet the shade of his father, Anchises, who showed him all his future royal descendants, right up to the great Caesars, Julius and Augustus.'

'Well, that can hardly apply to us,' said Florence. 'My father's still alive. I'm not going to find him here.'

'I could find mine,' Ante brought out before she could stop herself. Heat rose up her neck as all eyes swivelled towards her. 'I mean,' she stammered, 'it's possible, isn't it? Like you said, Gil.'

But Gil looked away. Understanding dawned and she squirmed inside. 'Not in *Elysium*, of course,' she cried. 'He wasn't a hero or – or anything. Somewhere further on!'

'I am certain that you will *not* find your father further on,' said Penelope gently. 'And you will be glad of it.'

A shiver ran down Ante's spine. 'You mean if I did, he'd be – he'd be somewhere horrible…' she faltered. Her mind flew back to the blank, faceless people on the jetty. Better not to find him at all than to see him with that crowd. She swallowed, her mouth dry.

Odysseus cleared his throat. 'There are – as I know

well – other reasons why a mortal might visit the Underworld. Perhaps you have a task to do?'

'Well, if we have, we don't know what it is,' said Florence.

And between them, with much interrupting of each other, they told their story.

'So,' said Odysseus when they finished. 'One of you belongs here. There is no doubt about that. Although why he should be destined for this terrible place, instead of the gentler path on the other side of the Styx – '

'But this place isn't terrible, it's first-rate!' cried Gil. 'The meadows, the stream – all that's missing is the green mountain with the path going up, but I'm sure I'll find it somewhere.'

Florence frowned. 'What green mountain?'

Hector and Aeneas looked mystified.

But Odysseus shook his head. 'No mountain here,' he sighed. 'And these meadows are not for you. Only the great Heroes may reside in Elysium. You belong to a different age, with different rules. You must follow the path down wherever it takes you.'

All three looked at him in dismay. In her mind's eye Ante saw again the yawning blackness of Cerberus's cave and the bare, stony path that led into the darkening gorge...

'But it's not just Gil,' she murmured. 'We've got ourselves into this too. What's going to happen to us?'

'Second thoughts, Ante?' said Florence. 'Bit late for that.'

Ante felt the blood rush into her cheeks. 'That's not what I meant! Of course I want to stick with Gil.' She tried to catch his eye but he kept his head turned from her. 'I – I just – ' her voice dried up. It was coming out all wrong.

Penelope came to her rescue. 'You are wondering how you came to be here at all and I must confess, it puzzles me too. Apart from Elysium, Hades is a place of punishment. I cannot believe you have committed the crimes for which people suffer in the circles below, but then nor can I believe it of this young man either. Florence, at least, is safe; she carries the bough. Whether she can bring you back to the Upper World with her, well…'

The unfinished sentence hung in the air.

'But it was me who' – Ante felt Florence's eyes on her – 'I mean, we *both* picked it. So it's for both of us.'

'Perhaps.' Penelope's expression was unfathomable.

'But – but – ' Gil's eyebrows drew together. 'I don't understand. I haven't – haven't done anything wrong.' He flicked his gaze from one face to another and then to the ground.

Ante studied him. What could he have to hide? He'd hardly had the chance to live, let alone commit crimes.

'Well, maybe I have done some things…' Biting his lips, he jabbed the earth with his shoe. Then his head shot up. 'At least I haven't killed anyone!' he burst out.

Ante gasped. Was he trying to turn the heat on *her*? She stared down at the ground, hands clutched behind her back, fingers slippery with sweat.

'And Ante hasn't either. We haven't done anything. So what's this all about?'

Not her then. Not what he meant. The green blur at her feet sharpened back into blades of grass.

From somewhere above Penelope spoke. 'Then neither of you can be punished.'

'No.' Gil shook his head several times, as if shaking away all possibility.

If only she could be so sure. Her neck ached with the effort of staring downwards but she didn't dare look up, not now with all eyes upon her, one pair in particular…

'We could ask that lady we met before,' came Florence's voice. 'The one who knows everything about everybody. Couldn't we?'

The tension was broken. Ante let out her breath.

'Cassandra,' sighed Hector, exchanging a look with Aeneas. 'She'll know but she won't say. She had a bad time of it with all her prophesying. We never believed her, you see, so she gave up. Oh, she'll let us in on a few new ideas, for amusement's sake, like cricket and football and other sports, just to give us a change from wrestling and horse-taming and such-like – but that's all.'

Penelope drew something round and shimmering from the folds of her robe and held it out to Ante. 'You may not carry the bough,' she said, 'but here is something else that will help you.'

'Thank you,' said Ante, wondering how a ball of fine,

silvery-grey thread, however beautiful, could be helpful, yet fearing it might be rude to ask.

Penelope smiled as if she read her thoughts. 'This thread is unbreakable,' she said. 'It has been dipped in the Styx. Sharp blades, brute force, even fire cannot touch it. What you bind stays bound.'

'Oh, I see. Great, thanks.' Ante pocketed the thread, unable to imagine that she'd want to bind anything, but grateful for the gift. Florence stared at her, a hard look in her eye.

'Well, my young friends – ' began Odysseus.

He broke off. A delightful sound, sweeter than birdsong, yet low, clear and piercing, filled the air. Through the trees appeared a slight young man with delicate features, playing a lyre.

'Orpheus!' Odysseus cried, 'Just the person. Our guests need to be guided back to the path. You know where.'

'Oh please,' begged Ante. 'Can't we stay a bit longer?'

Hector and Aeneas glanced significantly towards the cricket pitch, where the players were gathering once more.

'I fear we have delayed you already,' said Odysseus. 'You may have a long journey – wait.'

He clapped his hand to his brow, turned and disappeared among the trees, returning a few moments later with three bulky shapes in his arms.

'Here,' he said, 'supplies for the journey. Drink it sparingly.'

Ante looked at what Odysseus had given her: a large, soft bag with a leather strap that she put across her shoulder. A seam sealed the white, furry material all the way along on one side, leaving only a small round opening at the upper end that had been stiffened enough to hold a cork. It felt heavy and something sloshed inside it. 'It's a kind of bottle!' she exclaimed.

Odysseus grinned. 'A kid skin, actually. Good for carrying water – something hard to find where you're going. Farewell, my young friends. Orpheus will look after you.' With a bow he was gone, Hector and Aeneas with him.

Sighing, Ante followed Florence and Gil as Orpheus led them round the cricket pitch.

'You know about where we're going, don't you?' asked Gil after a moment. 'From when you went through Hades. While you were still alive.'

'It is a dark path,' Orpheus replied, 'and there are many dangers. You will know when you have reached your goal.'

Ante grimaced. So much for their guide's firsthand knowledge.

They crossed the line of trees on the far side of the pitch and were half-way across the meadow when Gil tried again. 'Have you any idea what that goal might be? Because we haven't.'

'It may be a goal or it may be a task,' said Orpheus.

Gil groaned.

The grass began to shorten and grow thinner. Dank

marsh fog crept towards them, blotting out the scent of honey on the air. Only a few paces away now the crag stretched up, the dark gash of Cerberus's cave in its flank, the bare, stony path curving round its base before disappearing into nothingness. Ante's stomach tightened.

Suddenly Orpheus lowered his lyre and for the first time, looked them all straight in the eye. 'I can tell you only this. When the time comes, *don't look back*. Farewell.'

'What?' Ante stared after him.

'When what time comes?' asked Florence.

'Hm.' Gil gazed at the retreating figure, a wrinkle in his brow. Then he shrugged his shoulders. 'Well, here goes.'

CHAPTER TEN

The Multivice Complex

The warm light that bathed the meadow weakened the moment they set foot on the path and gradually, with each footstep, grew dimmer. Soon they were descending in a kind of twilight, the path growing narrower as it became steeper, until they could no longer walk three abreast. On their left a sheer rock face rose up higher and higher, while to their right the ground dropped away into darkness, so that they couldn't tell where the bottom of the gorge might be, but that it must be hundreds of metres below.

'Stop for a minute.' Ante hugged the cliff face. The waterskin pulled at her shoulder. Grit forced itself under her fingernails where she clung on, knuckles whitening, while the distance between her and the others grew with every second. How could they walk along so easily when one false step, one slip on the loose stones near the edge of the path… She shuddered.

'Are you all right, Ante?' Gil called back.

'I will be.' *Keep going.* 'Just a bit dizzy, that's all.'

'Let's take a break then,' said Florence. 'It's not like we're in a hurry.'

Sitting down, she leant back against the cliff. Ante inched her way over to her, sank to the ground and closed her eyes. That way she didn't have to look at the yawning chasm on the other side of the path.

'Ante, can I ask you something?'

'Sure.' She looked up. Florence had never spoken to her this nicely before. Maybe now they were thrown together…

'Can I see the present Penelope gave you?'

Feeling in the pocket of her skirt, Ante drew out the ball of fine, silver thread. It shone in the twilight around them, bright, but not as bright as the golden bough in Florence's belt. Like the moon and sun, thought Ante.

'Oh, isn't it lovely.' Florence stretched out her hand. 'Can I hold it?'

Ante stiffened. *Oh no you don't, Florence. Not this time.* 'No.'

Gil, leaning back against the cliff with his hands in his pockets, looked down sharply. 'Hey, that's a bit mean, Ante. She only wants to look at it.'

Ante curled her fingers around the ball. 'She can look at it.'

'Oh, come on, Ante, I'll give it straight back,' pleaded Florence.

'Yes, go on, what've you got to lose?' said Gil. 'Look, I know you two had some kind of row back in the organ loft, but we're all friends now, aren't we?'

'Penelope gave it to *me*.' Ante looked hard at the ground. 'It's *mine*.'

She winced as Gil snatched his hands from his pockets and towered over her. 'You know, I really don't know what to make of you,' he cried. 'One minute you're nice; the next you're selfish and possessive and sulky and mean and – '

'Don't go on at her, Gil,' said Florence in a small voice. Rising, she straightened her skirt. 'If Ante feels she can't trust me, it's up to her. It doesn't matter.'

She set off down the path again without another glance. Gil shot Ante a now-see-what-you've-done look and followed, leaving Ante to scramble miserably along behind.

It was growing darker. From somewhere in the distance came waves of noise, a mixture of loud music, rhythmic thumpings and, as they drew nearer, what sounded like somebody shouting through a loudspeaker. A sweet, sickly, familiar smell crept into the air, but Ante couldn't give her attention to any of these things; it was costing her all her strength and concentration to cling to the cliff side of the path and yet not lose sight of the others. The golden bough, bobbing in Florence's belt, cast its own pool of light; if she allowed it to get too far ahead, what was to stop her falling over the edge? Not that that possibility had occurred to *them*. And she certainly wasn't going to point it out.

At last, rounding a sharp corner, a blaze of lights made her screw up her eyes. Before her the path widened immensely, opening out into a huge plateau on the side of the gorge, holding what looked like a shopping mall. Built around three sides of a square, it was crowded with stalls and booths offering – ah, *now* she remembered that smell. The dirty polystyrene containers and smeared paper napkins, the crushed drinks' cans and plastic cups littering the ground, blowing along in the warm air – all told the same story. This was Fast-Food Heaven.

'You mean to say, you can *eat* all these things?' Gil shouted above the cacophony of canned music issuing from one of the buildings. In his hand he held an empty can, black, with *Demonade* written in a spiral of silver lettering around it.

Before Florence could reply, the music stopped and a voice boomed over the loudspeakers: 'WELCOME!'

Ante's gaze flew upwards. The lights, which had been running in patterns along the building on the far side of the square, formed themselves into words that echoed through the loudspeaker. She watched, open-mouthed.

'Welcome to… Hades – Is – Us! The Shopping Maul – yes that's M-A-U-L folks, we have a sense of humour here – To End All Shopping Malls! Well, to End Everything really… And the Magnificent Multivice Complex, incorporating – drum roll, please – THE SEVEN DEADLY SINS!'

The lights printed out the words in all the colours of the rainbow.

'Featuring, for your delight and entertainment – Gorgeous… GLUTTONY!'

This was spelt out in broad, rounded, pink lettering.

'Chilled-out… SLOTH!'

A sloping, sprawling script worked its way in grey lights across the building. It took some time.

'Eat-your-heart-out… ENVY!'

In green, of course.

'PRIDE!… AVARICE!… LUST!'

Each booming announcement was illustrated in colour, except for the last.

'Awesome… ANGER!'

The white lights sprang away and formed themselves around the lettering this time, so that the word appeared in large, jagged pools of darkness.

'Now then, come along, what's it going to be? A glimpse of Gluttony to begin with, perhaps?'

Ante stared at Gil and Florence. What were they supposed to do? She shifted her gaze to the square before her, packed with all kinds of people, from businessmen in crumpled suits to pale, flabby teenagers. They wandered between the burger, fish and chip and ice cream stalls, behind which a band of workers in black t-shirts and baseball caps turned out piles of soft, greasy, sticky things to eat. Yet instead of falling on the food – as from their sad eyes and wet, puffy lips they longed to do – nobody was eating anything. It was very strange.

'No, Tantalus.' A chef waved away a haggard man as

he lunged for the basket she was raising out of the fryer. 'No one will serve you, you know that.'

Florence looked at the crisp, golden chips and gave a charming smile. 'Can I try some? They look so – hey, what's the matter?'

For no sooner did she reach out and touch the chips than the girl dropped the basket and shot to the back of the booth, covering her head with her hands. Florence, Ante and Gil stood staring at her, uncomprehendingly.

Not for long.

A hideous screeching filled the air. People ran in all directions, wheezing and stumbling. A large, middle-aged man in a grubby vest and flapping Bermuda shorts bumped into Ante as he rushed past. 'Get away from there!' he panted over his shoulder. 'They're coming, can't you hear?'

'What – who – ?' cried Ante, as the screeching soared to an unbearable pitch.

'Duck!' The warning came from the fish and chip girl, cowering at the back of her booth.

Too late. Ante felt the breeze of powerful wings narrowly miss her head just as Florence let out a terrified scream. 'My *hand!*'

Blood trickled down the palm where sharp claws had wrested the chips from her fingers. A whirl of dark feathers and savage talons filled the booth as three huge birds landed heavily and began tearing at the food laid out there.

No, not birds.

Birds do not look up in the midst of their feasting and jeer spitefully through twisted lips at the people around them. Nor did any bird Ante had ever seen make such a disgusting mess as these creatures did, soiling the food as they ate it and leaving trails of excrement as they plundered one fast-food stall after another. What they didn't eat they slobbered over, turning the food bad instantly. The smell was appalling.

Ante covered her nose with her sleeve. 'What are they?' she gulped.

Beside her Florence clutched her bleeding hand. 'I think I'm going to be sick,' she moaned.

Gil looked pale. 'Harpies,' he said. 'Sort of half-vulture, half-girl, they swoop down on feasts and spoil everything they touch.'

The creatures spread their wings and took to the air, screeching as they soared away. Behind them lay a wasteland of filth and rotting bits of food.

'Was that my fault?' asked Florence, as the girl emerged from the back of her stall. 'Because I took some chips?'

The girl sighed. 'Every Glutton does it once. Mind you' – she shot them a quizzical look – 'you're the most restrained lot of Gluttons we've ever had. Usually they jump right in.'

'We're not gluttons!' protested Florence.

'No? What are you in here for then? Avarice? You should be in the Shopping Maul over there.' She pointed to the left of the square. 'Or Lust – clubbing with the Loving Dead in the building behind me. Though I'd say you were a bit young to *have* serious partners yet, let alone cheat on them.'

'*Serious partners*? What are you talking about?' asked Gil.

'OK, Sloth then? Daytime Television Lounge on this side. Your own personal least favourite TV programme played on loop for you all day and all night. No? Well if it's Pride then you can start right now with all the others.'

'*What*?' said Florence.

'Start what?' said Ante.

'You don't understand – ' began Gil.

The girl wasn't listening. 'Come along, get on with it,' she called, but not to them.

From a gateway in the far left-hand corner people streamed into the square. Sweeping past the little groups of Gluttons now emerging from the Maul in which they'd taken refuge, these new arrivals couldn't have looked more different, with their straight backs and haughty expressions. The mops and buckets they carried, clearly unwillingly, hardly matched their arrogant air, nor did their rather strange clothes.

'These guys – what are they *wearing*?' murmured Florence.

Ante followed her gaze to where a fair-haired young woman forced herself, with evident disgust, to pick up the rotting remains of food left by the Harpies and put them in a black bin bag. She wore a frilly, floral cotton dress, trimmed with a big white collar and a pink sash.

'I wouldn't be seen *dead* in a dress like that,' squeaked Florence.

A silence fell. People stopped their clearing and mopping and turned to look at them. The woman in the floral dress straightened up and glared at Florence.

'Oh, wouldn't you?' Her voice was like splinters of glass. 'Well, let's just see what you will be seen dead in, shall we? School uniform, is it? You ugly little brats must have done something really terrible to have earned your place in this dump – oww! Yeuggh!' A generous spadeful of Harpy mess hit the woman full in the face and the spiteful tone instantly gave way to wailing.

'Bullying children now? Even the Harpies aren't as disgusting as you, Karen.' Next to Ante, the fish and chip girl stood leaning on a spade, eyes blazing. 'What have you got to be proud about? Your looks? Not really. Your clothes? Don't make me laugh. Now, get back to work, all of you! And that,' she added, turning to the three of them, 'goes for you too, so come on – oh.' Her eyes fell on the golden bough in Florence's belt.

She gave a low whistle. 'What's this, then – tourism? Come to get a feel for the place before committing yourselves, perhaps?'

Florence glared at her. 'What makes you think we *wanted* to come here?' she snapped. 'It's not our fault – '

'We don't know why we're here, actually,' Ante broke in as a glassy, world-weary look entered the fish and chip girl's eye. 'But we are. And if Gil' – she nodded at him – 'has to make this journey, then we're going too.'

Setting her mouth firm, she glanced at Florence. *See. No second thoughts, whatever you think.* Florence lifted one eyebrow but said nothing.

The girl's gaze travelled from Ante to Gil and back again. 'Well, he doesn't belong in this circle,' she said. 'So you'll all have to go on. See that building behind me?'

'The one with the coloured lights? And someone talking through loudspeakers?' Ante found herself shouting as the canned music, silent during the invasion of the Harpies, blared out once more.

'In that building,' said the girl, ignoring her, 'is the Club of the Loving Dead. Go through it and on the other side you'll find the path down to the next circle. No one is supposed to get out, of course, but with that bough I don't think you'll have any trouble.'

Turning, she walked back to her fish and chip stall.

'Doesn't anyone ever get out of here?' Ante called after her. 'If they haven't got a return ticket, that is?'

'No. Yes. Maybe. Sometimes some of them begin to see beyond themselves – once in a thousand years perhaps.'

This didn't sound hopeful. Ante sighed and turned to follow Florence and Gil, already making their way across the square.

'Wait!' The fish and chip girl shouted above the

canned music. 'That bough – I'd keep it out of sight around here if I were you.'

'Why?' asked Florence.

But the girl didn't reply, or if she did it was lost in a tremendous hissing sound as she plunged the basket of fish into the bubbling fat.

CHAPTER ELEVEN

Chains of Gold

'No way,' said Florence, tucking the bough under her sweatshirt before pulling it out again. 'It looks stupid.'

Ante glanced around them, wondering what the girl had meant. One or two of the Proud stopped to stare at this beautiful golden ornament as they passed; the Gluttons, wandering hungrily from one fast-food outlet to another, took no notice at all.

But now another kind of person appeared in the square. A couple of men in dark suits hovered near the shop windows, glancing at the goods before moving on. Their sunglasses should have given them a holiday air; yet there was nothing relaxed about the way they stooped, breathing hard, as if bearing huge burdens on their shoulders – which indeed they did, for large gold chains lay around their necks and wrists, cutting into the flesh, rendering it sore and swollen. *Ouch.* Ante's own shoulders and arms ached in sympathy as she watched the men walk laboriously past the Proud, who, having finished their task, clustered around the windows to gaze at the range of designer clothes and accessories they contained.

'Oh, *look*,' breathed Florence, 'that dress!' Before either Gil or Ante could stop her, she ran and pressed her nose to the glass in front of a long, slim-cut evening dress in the palest pink silk. 'Wouldn't that look great on me?' she cooed.

The two men looked up. Under their sunglasses Ante sensed a flicker of interest, hunger even; and they weren't the only ones. From all sides sharply-dressed men and women, weighed down with chunks of gold, made for the shop window. Ante looked at the circle of faces – expressionless save for a slight parting of the lips, a gleam of saliva on the tongue – and stiffened.

'Good day, young lady.' A flash of very white teeth. 'Nice dress, isn't it?'

'Beautiful,' sighed Florence.

'Would you like it?'

'Oh, can I?' She spun round to look at the man. 'But how? I don't have any money.'

'Florence – ' Gil began.

'That can be arranged.' A new voice, smooth and cold as stone, caused Florence to turn again. It belonged to a slender, honey-blonde woman in a leopard-skin dress and tight gold sandals. She too wore heavy gold chains around her neck and wrists but apparently these weren't enough, for a thick golden belt, studded with diamonds, cut into her slight hips and a band of gleaming metal imprisoned each of her ankles. 'You have something I could give you many rootofevils for. More than enough to pay for the dress.'

'Roota-*what*?' said Gil, as Florence stared at the speaker.

'Rootofevils,' repeated the woman. 'It's the currency here. That dress, for instance, costs 250 ROEs, as you can see. Now, you happen to be wearing a most elegant buckle on your belt but – please don't take this the wrong way – isn't it rather an awkward shape? Tell you what, I'll give you 300 ROEs for it. Then you can buy the dress and have something left over for your friends, maybe.'

Her smile extended to include Gil and Ante in its spiky embrace.

'No, sorry, I can't do that,' said Florence. 'You see – '

'No, you certainly can't,' interrupted the man with the teeth. 'Hey Steph, what the hell do you think you're playing at? Three hundred lousy ROEs? You'll give Avarice a bad name, you will. That fancy bit of bling is worth at least 400. In fact,' he turned to Florence, his voice dropping to a warm, fatherly tone, 'I'll tell you what I'll do. I'll make it 450. That's more than it's worth, you know that, but I want you to be happy.'

He stretched out his hand to the bough.

'No!' Florence grabbed her belt and leapt back out of range. 'It's not for sale!'

'Come on, Florence,' said Gil, taking her firmly by the arm, 'we're leaving. *Now.*'

He steered her through the crowd of suits and gold.

Ante, not daring to take Florence's other arm, pressed as close as she could. Together they forced a path back to the centre of the square.

'At least we offered to *buy* it off you,' the woman called after them. 'Others might not.'

'What does she mean?' asked Ante.

'I think I know,' replied Gil grimly. 'Look.'

Between them and the building ahead, richly-dressed men and women, all dripping with gold, were gathering in small groups. Hands in their pockets, the men tapped their feet to the music from the loudspeakers as if totally absorbed in it; yet there was something watchful and tense about their posture, shoulders squared in defiance of the chains weighing them down.

Tense – like panthers, ready to pounce. And more of them were arriving all the time.

'I don't like this,' wailed Florence. 'We have to go through them *again*. And there are hundreds of them now.'

'We should be safe with the bough, though, shouldn't we?' said Ante.

'Yes, but suppose one of them makes a grab for it?'

'All of them, more like. They're obsessed with gold,' muttered Gil. He studied Florence for a moment. 'It's too late to hide the bough. What we need is to fix it to you somehow, really firmly, so that no one can – hey, I've got it! Ante,' he swung round to her, '*this* is what it's for! The silver thread Penelope gave you – we can use it to tie the bough to Florence's belt. *What you bind stays bound*, remember? No one'll be able to take the bough from her then.'

'Oh, Gil, that's brilliant,' cried Florence. 'Quick, Ante!'

Two pairs of eyes, glowing with expectation, met Ante's. Her hand went to her pocket – and stopped. At the back of her mind something spoke. *This is not what the thread is for.*

It was one of the hardest things she'd ever had to do. 'No.'

'*What?*' Gil looked as if he couldn't believe his ears. 'Ante, this is important, can't you see? This is for all of us! Can't you stop being selfish for once?'

Ante plunged her hand into her pocket and gripped the smooth ball of thread. Tears gathered in her throat.

'Gil's right, Ante,' hissed Florence. 'It's the only way. Look, I'm sorry we're taking your precious treasure off you but – '

'It isn't,' said Ante, swallowing hard.

'Isn't what?' asked Gil.

'It isn't the only way. Who says it's the only way? The bough is meant to protect us, isn't it? So why should those guys over there be able to steal it? *If you steal to make your gain, nothing will it bring but pain*, that's what it said on the tree. Or don't you believe it anymore?'

Gil and Florence looked at each other.

'It's just – it's just that I'd feel safer if we could tie it on somehow,' said Florence. 'Please, Ante.'

Ante couldn't meet her eye. 'I'm sorry,' she mumbled.

'I – I just know it would be a waste. Of Penelope's gift, I mean. I can't explain why.'

'Yes, well, I think we understand why,' said Gil. 'Using it to help your *friends* would be a waste, that's what you mean.'

'No, Gil.' Heat rushed into her eyes, blurring her vision. 'It's *not* – ' words choked her and she couldn't go on.

Gil took Florence's hand. 'Right,' he said, 'at least we know where we stand. We'll just have to brave it out, that's all.'

Ante crumpled. 'Gil, *please* – '

But Florence and Gil struck out towards the building without giving her another look.

Behind them, the dark-suited sharks closed in.

CHAPTER TWELVE

The Loving Dead

'Not you, little girl.'

Three tall, thick-set men barred the way. Blinking hard, Ante craned round to see if – *yes.* Florence and Gil hadn't been stopped. There they stood, at the door of the Club of the Loving Dead.

'Let me through,' she panted. 'I'm with them.'

'Oh, *with* them, are you?' replied the tallest man. 'That's not what it looks like from here.'

Behind him Ante could just see the door beginning to open. A shaft of crimson light fell across the ground, outlining the man's raised arms in a red glow, giving him a diabolical look. Thumping club music poured out of the door, matching what was blaring from the loudspeakers. She lunged forward.

'Oh, no you don't.' The man caught her easily. 'The Loving Dead is no place for the likes of you.'

'But I have to go! I have to be with my friends! Let me past – *please* – '

It was no use. Two powerful hands pinned her arms to her side, the gold chains round their owner's wrists pressing into her bones. She yanked her head back to plead with him, implore, beg, whatever it took, but he barely noticed. He was looking at his neighbour and laughing. '*Friends* she calls them! Hear that, Dan?'

'Yeah,' grinned Dan. 'That's good, that is.'

'OK, so maybe they're not my friends exactly – '

'That's more like it.'

' – but I must go after them, I must!' She felt her voice rising to a shriek. Behind the men the red shaft of light disappeared as the door closed. Straining round the arms that barred her way, she could see no sign of Florence and Gil.

'Now there's an admission,' said the man. 'You *must* go after them, must you? Won't leave them alone, even among the Loving Dead? If I ever heard one of the Envious condemn herself out of her own mouth – '

'Envious?' What was he talking about? 'Loving De– oh, I see! You think Florence and Gil are in love? And that I'm *jealous* of them?'

It was too absurd for words. She began to laugh. 'Of course they aren't. They're much too young. And I'm not – '

'Say what you like,' he cut in. 'But it was pretty clear to us. A couple comes along, hand in hand, they're in a hurry, they make straight for the Club. Then you turn up hard on their heels, all sulky-like. Now, if they was really your friends, they'd've waited for you.'

Ante stopped struggling. Her limbs seemed to turn to lead.

'So, do us all a favour,' he continued. 'Get back into the Maul with the other Envious and go on counting all the things everyone else can buy and you can't. Like my handsome jewellery I see you have your eye on.'

Blood rushed into Ante's cheeks. He'd got it all wrong! The clanking gold fascinated her for its sheer ugliness, for the pain given to flesh swelling inside its grip – how could she want that? And as for being envious of Gil and Florence… That wasn't the point. The point was to go after them, not to be left behind –

A sound rent the air. Piercing – and strangely familiar. The hands holding her arms dropped. Ante ducked, pressing her fingers to her ears, as Harpies swooped over her head, dive-bombing the food stalls. People ran everywhere and in the confusion, Ante seized her chance. She dashed for the door and pushed it open.

It was like entering a huge, high-ceilinged cave. A crimson glow bathed numberless shapes that jerked and writhed to the dance beat echoing off invisible walls. As her eyes adjusted to the strange light, the shapes sorted themselves into hundreds of dancing couples, wearing costumes representing every age in human history. The mother of all fancy dress balls, thought Ante, threading her way through them.

'Sorry.' She blundered into a slim, elegant lady who sprang away from her partner and glared at her. Her eyes, large and beautiful, were accentuated by eyeliner. Her thick, glossy black hair skimmed her shoulders, with a severe fringe across her brow, and around her head coiled a thin snake made of gold, its head raised in the centre of her forehead, as if ready to strike.

'Wow!' said Ante. 'You look just like Cleopatra!'

'What do you mean, *like*?' snapped the lady. She turned to her partner, a battle-scarred warrior in full Roman armour, a red cloak cast loosely around his broad shoulders. 'Mark Antony, remove this impertinent slave. As if having to dance perpetually to this infernal rubbish were not enough, must I endure insults as well?'

'Intolerable,' agreed the warrior.

Yet again strong hands seized Ante, pushing her back to the entrance of the building, away from Florence and Gil. 'No, no, you don't understand!' she cried, grappling with the man's wrists, her fingers sliding off metal, 'I must catch up with my friends, we mustn't be separated or I'll lose them!'

'Separated? Who talks of being separated?' A girl in a floor-length dress turned to look at Ante. She had long, red-gold hair that fell to her waist, and large, frightened eyes. A young man encircled her protectively with his arm while she entwined her arms around him, as if fearing he might be snatched from her at any minute. 'They're not going to separate us, are they?'

'No, Francesca,' replied Mark Antony, giving Ante a final shove, 'you and Paolo are quite safe. And you,' he glared at Ante, 'get out. This is no place for an avenging fury determined to pursue her victims, even after death.'

'*Victims*?' cried Ante. 'They're not my victims! I only want to catch up with them, I – '

'Poor things,' murmured Francesca. 'So young, too. No wonder they were in such a hurry to get away.'

Ante's eyes flew to hers. 'You've seen them, then? Which way did they go?'

'Do you think we'd tell you that?' burst in Paolo. 'What are you doing here, anyway? You should be down below. With the murderers!'

'*Murderers*?' It was like a shock of cold water. For a moment Ante was speechless. 'No, no it's not like that at all,' she spluttered. 'I promise – '

She broke off. Ahead something flashed. Something bright and gold, lost again immediately in the crowd.

'Sorry, no time to explain!' She leapt forward, pushing past the astonished Paolo and Francesca. Ignoring cries of indignation from all around, she barged through the couples now sliding over the floor to a sleepy love song, and made for the far side of the building. 'Wait! Florence – Gil – wait for me!'

It was hopeless. The sickly-sweet wave of music pouring from somewhere high above drowned her voice. She pushed her way on and now at last caught a glimpse of the back of Florence's blonde head. Beyond, raised high, a ray of gold shone through the crimson light...

'Florence, no! Wait – oh *please*!'

At the touch of the bough the wall opened just wide enough for Florence and Gil to slip through. With one last effort Ante hurled herself after them.

Her arms hit unforgiving rock.

CHAPTER THIRTEEN

Chiron

For a moment she couldn't move. Ridges of stone pressed her cheek, her elbows, her knees… she shifted position and yelped as numb areas flooded with pain. Slowly, clenching her teeth, she got to her feet.

They'd gone. They really had gone. Left her behind in a place she could never escape without their help. She ran her eyes over the wall searching for even the tiniest crack, but in vain. The rough, blank surface stared back at her.

Turning, she stumbled back the way she'd come, not caring how many couples she bumped into, not caring about anything because nothing mattered anymore. Not in the face of the one bleak certainty filling her mind to bursting point.

They'd deserted her. From Florence this was no surprise. But from Gil – it was like being stabbed in the heart. *I only have myself to blame* rang over and over in her brain. She'd irritated him, she'd said and done things he found inexplicable – but she never dreamt he actually hated her, hated her as much as Florence did, hated her enough to want to lose her as fully and finally as this. Tears rushed into her eyes and down her cheeks, trickling inside her shirt collar. Blinking through a crimson haze she fumbled for the door.

In the square all was confusion: tables overturned and food scattered over the ground. On several of the stalls the awnings fluttered in tatters and at least two had been destroyed completely, their contents smashed under heaps of twisted metal and splintered wood. There was no sign of the fish and chip girl and her companions, nor of the sharp-suited Avaricious, nor even of the herds of Gluttons who normally strolled around so mournfully. At last she spotted some of them, cowering against the windows of the Shopping Maul. Not such a good place to take refuge, as it turned out.

For in the square itself seethed a crowd of people unlike anybody Ante had ever seen. Huge figures with bulging muscles aimed blows at everyone who got in their way, roaring and snarling like wild beasts. There were men and women of all races and ages, wearing scraps of clothes – from vests and jeans to full brown army uniforms – so tattered they were hardly recognisable. Some of the men had long flowing hair and beards, some wore their hair cut very short, while others were completely clean-shaven. Ante watched in horror as, unable to find anyone left in the square to terrorise, they set upon each other, tearing at flesh with their bare teeth.

Now from the gateway to her right, through which the Proud had come and gone with their bin bags and buckets, there came a drumming of many hooves on the ground. The gate swung at a crazy angle, as if it had been forced open; as the drumming grew louder, it began to shake on its hinges. The next moment flashes of chestnut brown cut through the angry crowd, hooves reared up and crashed down, forcing the knots of fighters to break apart from each other. Roars of frustration met stern commands as about a dozen horsemen rounded the rioters up. When a couple managed to break away and make a dash for the Shopping Maul, two horsemen raised bows and pointed; the runaways lurched forwards into the windows as an arrow struck one in the back, the other on the shoulder. Ante screamed as glass splinters flew everywhere, cutting and grazing some of the poor Gluttons who hadn't got out of the way fast enough, as well as the two runaways, who in their rage seemed to feel no pain at all. Instead, they allowed themselves, spitting and cursing, to be herded back with their fellows to the corner of the square.

But her scream hadn't gone unnoticed. As the tallest and most muscular of the horsemen turned to look at her, Ante couldn't repress a gasp of amazement. For these were horsemen indeed: tall and strong with long, thick brown hair and beards, their deeply tanned skin naked to the waist; while from the waist down they were horses of a deep chestnut colour, with soft, gleaming coats and shining hooves.

The horseman studied her for a moment before walking in her direction until his smooth, glossy coat was only an arm's length away.

'Go on, then.' The voice was deep and rich.

Blushing (had she made it that obvious?), Ante reached out and stroked his flank. The hair felt soft and warm, just like a normal horse.

He closed his eyes. 'Long time since anyone's done that,' he sighed. 'So,' he said, looking down at her, 'what am I to make of you? You don't look like a Glutton or an Avaricious, you can't be one of the Lustful or you'd be in there, clubbing with the others – and you don't strike me as one of the Angry. I'd say you've never even seen a centaur before.'

'A centaur? Is that what you are?'

'That is what we are.'

He nodded towards the gateway in the corner of the square, through which the last of the rioters were being coerced by two of the horsemen.

'Our task is to keep control of the Angry – not always easy. They break out every now and then, but we soon round 'em up again. Leaves a horrible mess though,' he added, surveying the wreckage. 'Still, not for long.'

Ante's heart jumped as the gate swung open again. But there was no sign of the snarling mob; instead an orderly stream of the Proud emerged, armed with buckets and bin bags as before. The centaur watched as they began to tackle the mess.

'So,' he turned back to her, 'where do you fit in? You look far too wide-awake for one of the Slothful, so that only leaves – '

'I'm none of those things,' she said hastily. 'I'm – well, I seem to be on a journey, but I don't know where to. There were three of us, you see, and Florence was carrying the golden bough – '

'The bough? Did you say the *golden* bough?'

She stopped at the sharpness of the interruption. He towered above her, eyes fixed on her face.

'Are you really talking about a golden bough?' he repeated. 'Plucked from the ilex in the heart of the wood on the bank of the Styx?'

'I – I think so,' she stammered. 'That's where we found it. It's our return ticket – well, for me and Florence, that is, I don't know about Gil…'

The centaur listened, head bowed, as she told her story. But at the mention of Elysium, his face lit up and she had to pause while he trotted back and forth in front of her. 'You went to Elysium? Then you saw some of my pupils. Tell me, how are they? Do they fight and shoot as well as ever?'

'Who do you mean?' Ante wondered. 'We saw lots of heroes there. Which ones?'

'Which ones? *You ask who was taught by Chiron?*'

She looked blankly up at him.

'Does my name mean nothing to you?' he cried. 'Don't you learn history at school? Achilles, Aeneas, Heracles – they would be nowhere without me! I taught them fighting, archery, horsemanship, music, medicine – everything they know.'

'We saw Aeneas,' said Ante quickly. 'He wasn't – er –

fighting, exactly.' Did cricket count as fighting? 'But he's a great batsman – I mean, warrior.'

Chiron seemed satisfied. He nodded to her to continue her story.

'Go on,' he commanded, when she came to a stop.

'That's it.'

'That's it? You mean they went on without you? *They had the golden bough and they left you behind*?'

His tone took her by surprise. She felt like a small child being asked to explain why her classmates had covered the blackboard in rude words. She could only nod as he strode back and forth around her, so that she had to turn this way and that to follow him.

At last he stood still, breathing fiercely. 'How could you let that happen?'

'Me?' she said dazedly. '*Let* it?'

'You are the bearer. Not Florence.'

'But according to her, we both – '

'No! Not according to her!' His voice echoed round the square, drowning the sickly music once more pouring from the loudspeakers. 'It doesn't work like that. The bough entrusts itself to one bearer only. That bearer would *never* abandon her companion, however much she disliked her. Yet you allowed your precious gift to fall into the hands of someone who would.'

'I didn't *allow* it,' cried Ante. 'She took it! And she wouldn't give it back.'

'In other words,' sighed Chiron, 'she stole it. She spun Gil a whole lot of nonsense about your *both* plucking the bough. And you didn't even try to put that right – '

'No, because he wouldn't have believed me!'

' – which means that Gil and Florence have carried on into the heart of Hades with nothing to protect them but an ordinary stick.'

'You mean' – Ante's voice faltered – 'because I'm not with them, the bough won't work anymore? And they could be in some sort of trouble?'

'Trouble? *Trouble*?' He leaned down and laid his hands on her shoulders. The grasp was strong and firm but not unkind. 'Listen to me, Ante.'

Something in his voice made the hairs rise on the back of her neck.

'Can you remember what it said on the ilex? About what would happen to anyone who stole the bough?'

'A – a crimson stream,' she mumbled, 'and – oh yes, some "kindly ones" coming to their aid. It didn't sound too bad, and if someone was going to help – '

'No!' Chiron almost pushed her away. He took a few steps back, his hooves clattering on the flagstones. 'The Kindly Ones will not help them. Don't you know who they are? The *Kindly Ones*! The Eumenides, daughters of the Night! Avenging Furies who punish people for their crimes, who hound and hound their victims until all life is sucked out of them and death is no release; they thrive on blood, guilt, pain and terror – no, no, it would be better to starve eternally with the Gluttons, or be crushed with gold like the Avaricious, or even to be torn apart by the Angry, than to be in the hands of Megara, Tisiphone and Alecto.'

He paused, hands on hips, staring down at the ground.

Ante opened her mouth. *Serves them right!* she wanted to yell. But the thought died as soon as it formed. In its place a black chasm yawned, releasing hideous creatures to shadow two small, solitary figures walking down a rocky path. A gathering of speed, a sudden snarl and the figures spin round, terror etched on their faces...

A shudder ran down her back. 'Is – is that it? These creatures – these Furies will find them and – and punish them? Forever?'

Chiron gazed at the Club of the Loving Dead, as if he could see through its solid walls to whatever horrors lay beyond. 'That depends,' he murmured.

The blood beat in Ante's ears. 'On – what?'

'On you.'

'On *me*? I've got to go to their rescue?'

'You have to regain the bough if you are ever to get home. What else you choose to do with it is up to you.'

'You mean, I could get the bough back off Florence – and then leave her and Gil behind?'

Chiron shrugged. 'They abandoned you.'

'Yes, but – ' she hesitated. *That would so turn the tables on Florence!*

And Gil.

'No.' She pulled herself up. 'I couldn't do that. Not if it's as bad as you say.'

Chiron's stern features broke into a smile. 'Spoken like the true bearer!' he cried. 'Come.'

She caught her breath as he wrapped his strong arms around her, lifted her off her feet and set her down astride his warm chestnut back.

'Put your arms round my waist,' he called over his shoulder, 'and hold on. There's no time to lose!'

CHAPTER FOURTEEN

The Fortress of Dis

Wheeling round, Chiron broke into a trot, heading across the square towards the gateway by the Shopping Maul.

'Wh – where are we going?' Ante squeezed the words out between jolts. It felt like sitting on an extremely hard chair that was suffering from hiccups.

'To the Kingdom of Dis, the place of Deliberate Sin. Where your friends are heading, if they haven't already arrived.'

'The place of *what*?'

'Deliberate Sin. All the people here in the Multivice Complex,' he waved his arm across the square, 'are paying for their selfishness, whether over money, status, possessions, desires – they don't set out to harm their fellows, they just don't think about them. But a person who plans in cold blood to damage another, to hurt them, to cheat them, or worst of all, to betray them, well – that's something else.'

Chiron slowed to go through the gateway and trotted down a narrow alley between the Shopping Maul and the Club of the Loving Dead. After the bright lights of the square it took Ante's eyes a moment to adjust to the gloom. The relentless throbbing of the music dropped and she began to be aware of different sounds ahead, above the clip-clopping of the centaur's hooves on the path. Screams and yells of rage, accompanied by loud sucking, squelching noises, drifted from the far end of the alley.

The alley opened out on to a large area of open ground sandwiched between the Club and the cliff face on the left. At least, the ground would have been open if it hadn't been taken up almost entirely by a long, stinking, muddy ditch. Wallowing up to their waists in slime, engaged in thrusting each others' heads down into it and bellowing with rage, were the Angry, watched over by the troop of centaurs, who patrolled the edge, firing arrows at any who tried to get out. As Ante stared, a group of the Proud appeared and calmly poured the contents of their bags and buckets into the writhing ditch.

'So this is where they came from!' Ante exclaimed. 'Ugh.'

A handful of mud hit her left leg and spattered across the centaur's gleaming coat. Chiron snorted but continued along the narrow strip of ground between the ditch and the Club, towards what looked like a dead end, where the building finished in a solid wall of rock that curved round into the cliff face. They were enclosed on all three sides.

'How will we ever – '

But just as they seemed to be heading straight into the cliff, a deeper patch of darkness appeared in the rock. Ducking slightly, Chiron plunged into it. Ante caught her breath.

'Your friends took a short-cut through the Loving Dead,' he explained, and the walls of the tunnel gave back his voice in a rich, deep echo. 'This is the more usual route. It will bring us out on the path further down.'

Ante clung on tightly, expecting every moment to scrape her arms on a jutting out piece of rock.

'Do the Angry ever try to escape this way?' she asked after a moment or two of silence broken only by the gentle thud of hooves on soft earth.

'Where to? Things do not get better as you go down in Hades. Even the Angry, mad as they are, know that.'

His words struck a chill in her heart. She hugged his waist, drawing strength from the feel of his solid, warm body in the circle of her arms. Closing her eyes, it wasn't Chiron anymore but *him*, and her arms were shorter and chubbier, she was jolting up and down on his back as he kicked piles of autumn leaves through the grass and they were both laughing…

The air around her lifted and she opened her eyes. They were out of the tunnel. Before her the path stretched into the gloom, winding ever round and down the gorge, its right edge falling sheer into a pool of darkness. Somewhere in those depths lay the Kingdom of Dis… A shiver shot through her and she gripped her hands more tightly together.

And yet – it didn't make sense. 'Chiron, can I ask you something? If these things – these Furies – are so terrible, why are they called the Kindly Ones?'

'It is a long story,' he replied. 'The people of Athens decided many years ago that, while they could never escape the forces of vengeance in the world, at least they could try and get them on their side. So they renamed the Furies the Kindly Ones and asked them to protect the city, to control anger and bloodshed so that the people didn't destroy themselves, but united against their enemies. It seemed worth a try, and as far as I know, Meg, Tissy and Alec quite liked the idea. But it doesn't change what they're there for. If you're not guilty of a crime, you don't have to worry. If you are – well,' he sighed, 'it wouldn't matter much what you called them. It wouldn't save you.'

His words rang hollow inside her. She fell silent, peering ahead, straining her eyes for a glimpse of gold round every outcrop of rock. But the darkness just grew stronger and thicker; it seemed to be pushing them back with a force that was almost tangible. Chiron's breathing quickened.

A red glow appeared ahead. It bled into the darkness, growing larger and sharper, outlining a vast, angular shape jutting out from the side of the gorge. It looked like a great, black fortress. Walls of stone blocked the path, soaring into battlements topped by jagged turrets, standing out black against the flickering light behind.

Flickering. Only one thing produced that kind of light. Even at this distance, she could feel the heat of fire on her skin.

'Is – is that Dis?' Dryness cracked her lips.

A single sound, a long, drawn-out wail, pierced the darkness. Ante reeled, nearly losing her balance. It came again, joined by others, rising and blending into each other in a howl that echoed and re-echoed around the gorge, part human, part – something else.

Inside her shirt she felt her skin prickle. 'What's that?' she whispered.

No reply. Only, against her arms, the muscles tensing in Chiron's back as he picked his way down the path whose twists and turns revealed more of the fortress in the blood-red glow. Weird how the flames must be dazzling her eyes to make her think pieces of the cliff were breaking off and…

Her stomach froze. This was no trick of the light. Shapes were separating from the rock face above and heaving up from the gorge below to crawl down the path in front of them. Strange, twisted shapes with webbed limbs like batwings, hooking their way across the ground, dragging filthy, ragged cloaks that caught and tore on sharp stones. Their faces, invisible under hoods, tilted upwards, as if sniffing the air.

Ante's insides turned to water. She clutched Chiron's waist with all her strength. 'Stop! Those things, whatever they are, they'll get us – *stop*!'

He did not even break stride. 'No,' he said. 'They have not been called for you.'

Not for you… but for someone else. As they rounded one more corner, Ante let out a scream.

Straight ahead stood the fortress. Under its walls huddled two figures – white-faced, lips parted – motionless save for their eyes, which darted over the mass of dark shapes swarming towards them.

'Quick, Chiron!'

Sweat poured down the centaur's body. Ante could feel his muscles straining but the uneven ground slowed him down. Up ahead the gap between the creatures and the cowering pair was narrowing fast.

From inside the fortress came a deep grinding sound. Ante ducked as a wave of heat rushed towards her; raising her head again, she gasped.

The huge fortress doors were opening. For a second the two figures stood outlined against a wall of flame; then Gil staggered as Florence collapsed against him. He yelled something Ante couldn't catch and pushed against Florence's frail, hunched-up form, forcing her upright. His hair clung to his brow as he struggled with her until at last her arm, raised more by his strength than hers, stretched upwards and brandished the bough.

Ante's heart turned over.

The bough gleamed, but not with gold. From the tip a dark stream snaked down, running over Florence's clenched fingers and down her bare arm, blood-red rivulets on pale skin…

Gil let out a cry and snatched his hand away. 'The crimson stream! But that means – and the *Kindly Ones*! Oh God, I remember now!'

Batwings clawed up his legs. A scream broke from Florence as a mouth, drawn wide to reveal small sharp teeth, clamped on to her neck, pulling her down. Other hooded figures piled in, clambering over each other, burying human limbs under a dark, seething mass.

Ante couldn't look. She pressed her face into Chiron's back. Under her cheek she felt his breath coming ever shorter as he pushed on to cover the last stretch of ground. *Faster, faster* hammered in her brain, the seconds feeling like hours.

He stopped. In the stillness Ante's sobs, stifled in her throat, rang out unnaturally loud.

The space before the fortress lay empty. Chiron stood, head bowed, sweat gleaming on his flanks, before the dark stone wall, unbroken save for the indent of the tall closed doors.

CHAPTER FIFTEEN

The Kindly Ones

Ante slithered off, her legs giving way as she touched down. She huddled on the hard ground, skirt twisted beneath her, dust stinging her cracked lips, while weakness swept through her like a wave.

They'd come too late. Those horrible creatures, those Furies, had dragged Gil and Florence inside the fortress and even now were tearing into their flesh, biting, clawing, *feeding*… A shudder racked her body, sending tears flooding into her eyes.

'Drink.'

'Wh-what?'

'Your water supply.' Chiron nodded to the kid skin, draped on the ground beside her.

She sat up. Pulling out the cork, she lifted the skin to her lips and let the warm, leathery liquid glide down her throat. That felt better. The tension in her muscles eased.

'Now tell me what you see.'

See? She looked about her. Red flames flickered from the battlements, sending shadows across the stone walls. Otherwise – nothing but darkness.

Not quite. Her eye caught a glimmer of gold at the foot of the fortress. With a cry she sprang forward. Warmth curled up her arm as the bough lay in her palm; smooth, clean, as if the crimson stream had never happened.

'So.' Chiron drew himself up. 'All's well then.' With a whisk of his tail he turned in the direction of the path.

'Wait.' Ante scrambled to her feet. 'Don't go, not yet!'

'I must,' he called back over his shoulder. 'I have been away from my post long enough.' Already beyond the reach of the firelight, only the skin of his back shone pale through the gloom.

She threw herself after him. 'Chiron, *please*! What do I do?'

'Follow the bough!' Hooves clattered up the path and faded away.

Ante let her arms fall to her sides, the memory of his solid, strong body still circled within them. *Gone. Him too.*

Darkness rolled up the gorge. At her back sheer, solid walls of stone, whose thickness concealed whatever terrors might be inside them; not a sound reached out here. But then the Furies had no more need to howl, with their prey in their grasp. Nausea filled her stomach and she staggered, grappling behind her for support.

A long, slow grinding noise. She spun round. The doors were opening, now they were coming for her! Reeling, she flung up her arms to protect her face.

Nothing happened. Light danced on the threshold as she lowered her hands.

Of course. It wasn't the Furies who'd opened the doors. The bough, held tight in her curled fingers, must have touched them as she'd fallen backwards.

Letting out her breath, she raised her hand. A blaze of gold lit up the darkness and seemed to race up her arm, through all her limbs, its warmth filling every corner of her body. *Yes.* This surge of energy, the bond that almost crackled between her palm and the slim shape that fitted it so snugly – this was how it should be. How it should have been from the start.

Sweat ran down inside her sleeve. Pulling off her jumper, she tied it round her waist and smoothed down her shirt. *So. Here goes.*

She stepped through the doorway into a heavy, lead-like silence. A passage led away into the gloom, lit up at intervals by fires that roared up the walls and blew gusts of heat towards her, making her gasp. Holding the bough steady she set off, trying not to notice the scuffling sounds coming from the deep shadows it cast; dark pockets perhaps where blood-thirsty Furies preyed on their victims.

She shuddered and the light wavered. But almost immediately her hand veered off to the left, steering her body to follow – *to follow the bough.* Yes! It was leading her to them, it must be! The outline of a doorframe, a heavy iron door opening slowly before her, firelight leaping across flagstones to reveal a black, distorted shape at the far end of the chamber…

Ante screamed. *The shape was moving.* Hooded creatures swarmed over each other in one seething mass. But as the bough's glow fell on them, they flung their heads back and scattered, shrieking, tattered cloaks flapping. With a breeze of their wings that lifted her hair, they streamed past her on either side and out of the door as she stood, shoulders hunched, arms clamped to her body, eyes shut tight.

Stillness fell. She opened her eyes.

On the floor lay a huddled figure. Bloodstained legs protruded from torn grey shorts and bleeding arms covered his face, as if to protect it from those gaping mouths.

Ante's arm shook, sending shadows darting up the cell walls. 'Gil,' she whispered.

No reply.

Creeping forwards, she crouched down, bathing him in light. 'Gil.'

A ripple of movement. She put a hand on his shoulder.

'Leave me alone!' He jerked away as if stung. '*Please* – I didn't want to do it, I swear! But he wouldn't – he wouldn't – *no!*' His voice rose to a shriek as he clutched his hands to his face.

'It's OK Gil, they've gone. It's me, Ante.'

Her heart beat fast. What was he raving about? The wounds were bad enough, but what had the Furies done to his mind?

'Ante.' Drawing his hands away, Gil blinked. '*Ante.*' Half-rising, he reached for her fingers as they slid from his shoulder and held them tight.

Relief rushed through her. 'Oh Gil, you're OK. I mean' – she looked down at her hand, now sticky with blood, and winced – 'you're hurt, but – '

'I'll be all right.' Grimacing, he pulled himself to a sitting position.

Ante breathed in sharply. All over his face, neck, hands, legs, wherever the skin lay open and easy to get at, tiny pairs of holes punctured the flesh. Bigger cuts showed where claws had scrabbled and found holds.

Gil met her gaze. 'Bloodsuckers,' he said. 'They don't want to destroy their victims, just – feed off them.' He closed his eyes. 'But they're gone now, thanks to you. However did you find me?'

She hesitated. It would take too long to tell him about Chiron. 'I followed the path till I found the bough. Or – it found me, I suppose.'

He nodded.

Ante suddenly found herself unable to look him in the eye. 'Gil, there's something I have to explain – '

'Don't,' he sighed. 'She stole it from you, I know. I just wish you'd told me. It – it would have made me understand things better.'

Ante flinched. She had steeled herself for his reproach. Not for this bewilderment. 'I know,' she whispered. 'I – I thought you wouldn't believe me. And it didn't seem to matter at first.'

'No – not until we left you behind! That was a rotten thing to do. I realised as soon as it happened but the wall closed and wouldn't open again. Florence reckoned it was because the bough only works forwards, not back, and we just had to carry on. Get help somewhere. Help, down here – how stupid could I be! Then the light began to fail and I couldn't understand why. Not until we got here and – ' he broke off, pressing his lips together. 'I'm sorry, Ante.'

She dropped her gaze. Her cheeks felt burning hot suddenly. Not from the fires. 'It's OK,' she mumbled.

'No, but it's worse than that.' Gil began, rather unsteadily, to get to his feet. 'I can't believe I swallowed her story so completely. She went on and on about how you had it in for her, ever since you stole something precious from her at *nursery* school, for heaven's sake.'

Ante gaped. 'I stole – what? What did I steal from her?'

He shook his head. 'She wouldn't say. That should've made me think twice but' – he sighed – 'it didn't. Nor the fact that she was so upset about it she made her parents take her away. Which is just silly! If it was that bad, you'd have been the one to leave, not her.'

Light pooled on the stone floor as the bough dangled in Ante's hand. She stared at the huge shadows, stretching and shrinking on the wall behind Gil's head, while his words rushed through her mind, joining with others in a different voice, mocking, triumphant. *Congratulations, scholarship girl. You just got yourself expelled.*

Was that what Florence was up to – revenge? But if so, *what for*?

A blank. Her mind could go no further. She wrenched it back to Gil, who'd started speaking again.

'You knew she'd get you back one day, she said, and you were scared, and that was why you lured her into the organ loft – '

'*Lured* her?' No, this was going too far!

' – so that she'd lean on the hand rail and – and – '

Ante couldn't breathe. She pressed her knuckles to her sides. 'And – *what*?' she whispered.

He bit his lip and flicked his eyes away, his pale, freckled skin flushed with red.

Heat spread up Ante's own neck and she bent her head, coils of hair falling forwards and hiding her face. *It's not true! She chased me in, I didn't lure her!* Setting her teeth, she tried to drown the voice that spoke unbidden in her mind. *But you didn't warn her, did you?*

Gil jerked round. 'Never mind, we've got to find her. Why she's been such a cow to you and landed us all in this mess I don't understand; but she's certainly paying for it now.'

The light blurred as he seized her arm and pulled her forwards. Steadying the bough, she felt a wave of anger. What a string of lies Florence had told! And yet – was there something behind it? Could she, Ante, have stolen some favourite toy or treasure when they were both little, and forgotten? Her brow ached as she tried to puzzle it out.

Gil tugged harder. 'She must be in here somewhere,' he panted. 'Quick, before it's too late!'

'Not so fast, Gil, you're hurt. Stop!' She raised her arm just in time to stop him crashing into the wall. 'It's no use. This is the end of the cell. And there's no sign – wait.'

To the right, the wall finished in a sharp, vertical line, beyond which lay a pool of blackness.

'A recess,' he muttered. 'Come on.'

They saw her legs first. Motionless, bloodstained. Ante's stomach froze.

It was worse than before. Gil had taken some shaking to come round, but only some. He hadn't lain completely still, eyes open and unblinking, his breath so faint it scarcely seemed to come at all.

'Florence.' Ante shook her, gently at first, then with increasing roughness.

No reaction. She took hold of the limp hands, wincing at the raw tears in the skin, and tried to pull her upwards. Gil's jaw tightened in pain as he crouched down on Florence's other side; tapping her face, he called her name over and over again. It made no difference. Wide open, the blue eyes stared into nothingness.

'She's in shock,' said Gil finally. 'I was afraid of that. I didn't think she'd be able to bear much of this.'

Ante fell back. 'So what do we do?'

'We get her out of here. Somehow.'

But as Gil, clenching his teeth, put one arm under

Florence's shoulders and one arm under her knees to lift her up, a tremor went through her body. He sat on his heels and watched as life seemed to return to her – at least, a kind of life. Palms on the ground, she sat up, facing straight ahead. Her gaze travelled over both of them with no sign of recognition. When she looked at the bough a flicker appeared briefly in her eyes, only to die, leaving her expressionless as before.

'Florence,' said Gil gently, 'it's me. Gil.'

'Gil,' repeated Florence.

'And – I'm Ante.'

'Ante.' The head turned slightly. Tendrils of hair clung to her neck in patches where the blood had dried.

Ante thought her heart would burst. If the mouth that barely moved had twisted and spat out her name, inches from her face, she couldn't have cared less – no, she'd be happy. Anything – even a chorus of Ante-Elephante – would be better than this lifeless figure that now sat in front of her. She never thought she'd find herself longing for the old Florence, standing here in this dank prison, watching Gil reach out a hand to help a shadow to her feet.

A shadow with Florence's delicate profile and slim form – and eyes that looked at you with no light in them.

CHAPTER SIXTEEN

The Burning Path

'Halt.'

Gil let out a cry and fell back; he would have knocked Florence off her feet again, had she not been standing as still as stone.

A dark figure towered over them, shaped like the hooded blood-sucking creatures that now gathered round its skirts like some monstrous brood, but taller, much taller. Red flames outlined the jagged folds of its long, black robes, torn and stained with blood, but the face under the dark hood was in deep shadow; or else it had no face at all. Ante could feel Gil trembling at her shoulder as it spoke again. 'She is ours. Look at her. Can you not tell?'

Feeling sick inside, Ante didn't trust herself to move, even enough to turn and look at Florence. She licked her lips. 'We can't leave her behind!'

'You cannot take her with you. The Kindly Ones do not give up their prey. She was warned; now she must pay for her crime. Do you think that just because you have the golden bough, you can play at Orpheus with his lyre? That you can you lead your precious friend through Phlegethon, River of Flame? LOOK AT HER!'

The sudden order made Ante jump. But before she could obey, Gil grabbed her shoulders and thrust his head close to hers, forcing her to keep looking straight at the Fury.

'No!' he shouted, 'don't look! *Don't look back.*'

'What?'

'Don't look at her,' he repeated. 'Start walking. It's our only chance.'

He steered Ante straight at the Fury who stood between them and the door of the cell.

'*Gil!*'

'Just hold the bough steady! You know it can't hurt you.'

The Fury let out a shriek. Long, pitiless fingers dragged at Ante's hair and shoulders to pull her back, but could not gain hold. A howl of frustration pursued the two of them into the corridor.

'Tisiphone! Alecto! Sisters, the *prey* – '

From deep within the fortress came an answering cry, followed by another, and then from all around voices joined in the same blood-chilling wail that had hounded them before. Ante shrank into herself, trying to block the sound.

The hands clutching her shoulders dug harder as Gil staggered. 'Ignore them,' he panted. 'Keep following the bough.'

She gasped. Ignore them? Leave Florence to the

swarming Furies and save their own skins, is that what he meant? 'No, Gil,' she yelled, twisting under his grip to try and look him in the eye, 'I will *not* keep following the bough, we are *not* going to leave Florence behind, Gil, how *could* you?'

'Ante, please, I know what I'm doing.'

'Yes, and so do I, you *coward* – '

'No! If you'll stop struggling for one second I'll explain – no, *don't* turn round!'

She paused, a lock of hair dancing before her eyes.

Gil went on, speaking very fast. 'If you can't promise me you won't I'll have to put my hands over your eyes and we'll go on walking like that, all the way. Understand?'

'Yes,' she replied sullenly.

'So do you promise – '

'Yes, yes, just tell me what this is all about!'

The ache in her shoulders lifted as he relaxed his grip. 'We're not leaving Florence behind,' he said. 'She's following us. No, don't look round! She's lost if you do!'

It felt as if her neck muscles might snap with the effort of holding still as Ante forced herself onwards. Ahead the corridor seemed to stretch into unending gloom; yet something had changed. Raising her head, she dared listen. *Yes.* The Furies' wailing still echoed round the walls but with a duller sound, as if receding into distance. She held her breath.

'It was when Megaera – the Fury – mentioned

Orpheus, it hit me,' said Gil. 'Orpheus's last words when he left us at the borders of Elysium.'

'He said...' Ante's brow furrowed. 'Oh yes. "Don't look back".'

'That's it! He was warning us. He'd been down here himself to find his wife, Eurydice, who'd been bitten by a snake and died. He played his lyre and charmed the Underworld so much that he was allowed to lead her back to life above again, but on one condition.'

'What? That he mustn't look at her? Just trust she was behind him?'

'Yes. And he nearly did it. He got right to the edge of Hades. Then he couldn't bear it any longer, he *had* to make sure.'

'He looked back!'

Gil nodded. 'She was there. She called out to him. He tried to grab her but he couldn't save her and she fell back down.'

Couldn't save her. Couldn't save her and she fell... The words tolled in Ante's mind. She swallowed hard, wincing as pain stabbed through her jaw, rendered rigid by the fight to hold her head still. For a while she walked in silence, taking as small steps as she dared, as if that alone would keep taut the invisible thread that bound Florence to their backs – if she was there at all and Gil wasn't making a terrible mistake and it was all some horrible trick...

'Ante.'

The hair rose on the back of her neck. Her hand

shook, tracing a golden blur in the darkness before them.

'Ante!'

Stronger this time. She breathed in sharply.

'Say nothing,' whispered Gil.

'But it's Florence!'

'Say *nothing*.'

She clenched her teeth, forcing herself to gaze fixedly ahead. The light and heat given out by the fires had been increasing steadily and she noticed with a shock that the ones they were passing now were much bigger than before: indeed, not far away they seemed to join together, right across the corridor itself.

'Ante – Gil – wait for me!'

'Keep going,' murmured Gil in her ear.

'Ante? Why – why won't you wait?'

A note of bewilderment crept into Florence's voice that pierced Ante to the heart. Closing her eyes she saw Florence standing alone, reaching out to her over an immense gulf.

'Is – is it because I left you behind? At that stupid Loving Dead place? Are you paying me back now? Please, Ante' – there was a break in her voice – 'please don't do this. Don't leave me in this terrible place. *Please*.'

She couldn't bear it. That Florence should think *that* of her, that she was playing some cruel vindictive game – no! She must tell her, Gil *must* let her – but his grip on her shoulders only grew tighter and his breath came in short gasps that almost burnt her cheek.

'Florence – is – following – us,' he said through gritted teeth, 'that's all that matters.'

'But she thinks I'm abandoning her, out of revenge!'

'Never mind what she thinks. Just keep going.'

Keep going? Her heart turned over. A wall loomed up ahead, made not of stone but of fire. It snaked across their path and far beyond it, like a river. A river of flame.

'Phlegethon,' muttered Gil, wiping his brow with his sleeve. 'Well, here goes.' Taking her firmly by the arm, he steered her straight into it.

Ante cried out. A blast of heat hit her face, tearing her hair in a stream behind her. Gil caught his breath and staggered, jerking them both off balance, but he pressed on into the flames. She screwed her eyes tightly, waiting for the searing pain she knew must come, the choking, frantic battle for air…

It didn't. The air was hot but she could breathe. Head down, she pushed against the strong, scorching wind. Beside her she glimpsed Gil's profile, outlined red in the firelight, his wide-open eyes reflecting the flames that parted as they walked through them. *Through them.* Ante's heart beat in her throat. Darkness, only a few paces away. They'd nearly made it.

Then, from behind, came a piercing scream. 'Ante, Gil! I'm burning, I'm *burning*! Stop, please stop! I *know* you can hear me! *Don't leave me to burn!*'

CHAPTER SEVENTEEN

Signs on the Wall

Ante wheeled round. Instantly two hot hands clamped over her face, the sweat stinging her eyes.

'Let go, Gil!' she yelled, rearing her head. 'We've got to get Florence, she's in pain!'

'If you think I'm going to allow you to wreck it all right now, when we're nearly through, you're making the biggest mistake of your life,' he shouted back. 'Now, face ahead and *keep going*. I'm not taking my hands off your eyes.'

What else could she do? Sobs racked her chest as she stumbled on, blind save for the red glow through Gil's palms. Eventually the glow darkened and cooler air fanned her cheek, the hot wind dropping behind her. Gil released his hold. Blurry-eyed and exhausted, she sank on to the hard ground.

'Hi.'

Her head shot up. She swivelled round on her knees, barely noticing the tiny stones scraping her skin.

A few paces away, outlined against the flames, sat a slight figure. Its face lay in shadow. Yet light from the bough caught a gleam in the eyes fixed on hers.

A gleam of recognition.

Waves of relief flooded through Ante. She flung herself at the figure, burying her head in its neck. 'Florence. Oh, *Florence.*' Her breath rushed out, flattening the ends of her bushy hair against the pale skin. 'Gil, you're a – a genius!' She choked and could say no more.

The thin shoulders stiffened under her touch. The chin jerked away. Ante raised her head. Eyes, large and blue, glittered in sunken sockets. Dry, swollen lips moved but no words came.

'Water,' panted Gil, from the ground nearby. 'She needs water. Badly.'

Crawling over to Florence, he removed the cork from her waterskin. She let the warm liquid touch her lips; she spluttered and gulped but finally drank deep, her eyes closed, her face relaxed.

After a moment he pulled the waterskin away. 'Enough for now. We mustn't use it all up.' With a sigh he sat back on his heels and drank from his own supply.

Ante followed suit. Letting her head fall back, she closed her eyes for a moment. They'd done it. Florence was shaken, her clothes torn, her skin raw and streaked with blood, but the blankness had gone from her expression. She was going to be OK.

Florence sat up and put her arms round her knees. 'Why is Gil a genius?' she asked. Her voice cracked slightly, still hoarse from the flames, but the words came out evenly enough. 'Did he rescue me?'

Ante nodded. 'Yes, he – '

'*What?*' Gil's eyes shot from Ante to Florence. 'How could I?' he cried. 'I was in the same fix as you, thanks to your scheming.' He paused, watching Florence.

Ignoring his gaze, she continued to look straight ahead.

'Ante rescued us both,' he went on. 'Though getting the Furies to release you was hardest of all, until I remembered about Orpheus and Eurydice. That's what Ante means.'

'Orpheus.' Florence echoed. A line furrowed her smooth brow, then cleared. 'Oh. I *see*. That's why you wouldn't wait. Or even turn round.'

'You know the story, then.'

'Of course.' She sank her chin on to her knees. 'I thought – but that explains it.' She pressed her lips together. 'It – it just wasn't very nice, that's all.'

There was an awkward silence. Ante looked down at the ground. Her hand tingled with the memory of how the slight shoulders had stiffened when she'd thrown herself at them just now. Shock, that was what she'd put it down to. That and the lack of water. Once recovered, Florence'd be shouting for joy at her rescue. Not brooding over the form that rescue had to take.

The hiss of a breath being let out sharply made her look up.

'Not – very – *nice*?' Gil glared at Florence. 'Would you rather she'd left you there? I can't believe I'm hearing this. After what Ante's been through for you, is that all you can say? You had plenty to say about her before, I seem to remember, all those lies about her stealing something of yours; when if anyone's a thief around here it's – '

'Stop, Gil.' Ante put a hand on his arm.

Florence's face had gone white. 'It wasn't the same!' Glancing at Ante, she snatched her eyes away, not quickly enough. Their stricken expression shook Ante to the core. 'I – I didn't mean to steal the bough! I thought I was l-looking after it.' A tremor went through her and she buried her head in her arms. 'I'm sorry,' she mumbled, the words muffled by her shirtsleeves. Then, even less distinctly, 'thanks, Ante.'

'It's – all right.' Ante looked down at the quivering blonde head while thoughts tumbled through her brain.

It was easy for Gil. Florence had lied about the bough, so nothing else she said could be true. Yet the look in her eye when Gil mentioned stealing – that was real enough. If she could only get to the bottom of this... She took a deep breath. 'It's – it's my fault a bit too. I – I should've been stronger and hung on to it. Not given in. According to Chiron, anyway.'

Florence's head lay still. Only the fingers clutching the elbows curled tightly. Was *that* it? Years ago, when they were both small, had Ante made Florence surrender something? If so, why couldn't she remember? Perhaps, with a bit more coaxing...

A cry broke from Gil. 'Chiron? The centaur Chiron?' He gazed at her, his eyes glowing, all anger forgotten.

'The one who taught Achilles and Heracles archery and swordsmanship and stuff? He's *here*? In Hades?'

The moment had gone. *Idiot, Ante.* She should've guessed the mention of the noble horseman who'd rescued her would fill Gil with excitement. 'Yes,' she said. 'At the Multivice Complex. He showed me another way to the path. Carried me, in fact.'

'*Carried* you? On his back? Oh, what I wouldn't give!'

She couldn't help smiling. 'It was a bit bumpy, actually. But he was kind. And – and he sort of said that the bough was my responsibility and it was up to me to sort things out. So – so that's what I did.'

She finished lamely and shot an anxious glance at Florence, just in time to catch the blue eyes resting on her. They looked away at once but Ante could have sworn their expression had softened. Something flickered in her chest.

'Good,' said Gil. His eye travelled from Ante to Florence and back again. 'Are you two done then? Friends?'

Ante hesitated. Florence stared down at the ground, the muscles round her mouth tense. Barely perceptibly, she gave a nod.

Ante turned to Gil. Her breath came out in a rush. 'Yes.'

'Well thank goodness for that.' Clapping his hands to his knees, he made to get up. 'And now the bough is back where it should be, I suppose we'd better – oh.' He broke off and stared at her for a moment.

'What?' said Ante.

'Nothing. I was just thinking: it's yours, the bough, not Florence's. That – changes things.'

Florence's face crumpled. 'Look, I've said I'm sorry. I'm not going to – '

Gil shook his head. 'Not what I meant. Forget it.' He got to his feet. 'Let's see where we are.'

Florence stood up and retied the sleeves of her sweatshirt around her waist. As Ante watched her – eyes cast down, mouth set in a little line – questions whirled in her brain. Did she mean it? Friends? It was hard to believe. Whatever Florence harboured against her, she was unlikely to let it go just like that. Easier to tell Gil what he wanted to hear.

Grimacing at the pain stabbing her ankles from the pressure of the hard ground, she rose and held up the bough. On one side, the River of Flame formed a barrier, cutting off any hope of a way back. On the other, the stone walls of Dis continued as uneven rock surfaces that stretched up and curved overhead, so that it felt like peering into a cave. No sign of a path anywhere. She let her arm fall. Light hovered over the stone floor, plunging everything else in gloom. For a moment she stood blinking into the darkness. In the panic of being abandoned, she hadn't thought beyond finding Gil and Florence. Now they were back together, what were they supposed to do? *Follow the path down wherever it takes you*, Odysseus had said. Was this it, then? Had Gil reached his destination here, in this dark and empty cave? If so, to leave him to it – well, that would be miserable enough. But – she glanced at Florence. The blue eyes left off scanning the flames, as if for a possible way through, and met hers. The same thought seemed to have occurred to her.

How were they to get back? What use was a return ticket if there was no way out?

'Hey, there's something here,' said Gil. 'Ante, look.' He stood leaning with one hand against the cave wall, beside a patch of total darkness. Close to, the darkness melted into jagged shapes of rock stretching far beyond the bough's glow.

'It's a tunnel!' Ante cried.

'Thought so,' said Gil. 'Let's go.'

'Wait,' said Florence. 'What's this?'

Ante turned. Firelight defined every tendril of Florence's hair and played on patterns of lines and triangles scratched into the rock wall above her hand.

'Looks like a sort of butterfly with a long tail,' said Ante, pointing the bough. 'There it is again – and another – they're all over the place. What d'you think they are, Gil?'

Gil didn't reply. He stood still, his head cocked. 'Did you hear that?'

'What?'

'*That.*'

From somewhere deep down the passage came a rumbling sound, so low Ante felt rather than heard it. Her eyes flew to Gil and Florence; they looked back, faces pale.

She tightened her fingers round the bough. 'We *have* to go that way. It must be the path, there is no other. Whatever that noise is – '

The rumbling stopped.

'Right. Here goes.' Squaring her shoulders and holding the bough straight before her like a drawn sword, Ante set off.

It was hard going. The tunnel twisted and turned so often she could never see more than a short way ahead; from the way it sloped, she guessed they must be descending the gorge once more. In several places the passage forked and openings to other tunnels kept appearing in the walls. Each time she had to test the way with the bough, following where it glowed brightest. It wasn't long before she'd lost all sense of direction.

'This isn't a path, it's a maze,' grumbled Florence. 'And I don't want to worry anybody, but that noise is getting louder.'

Ante stopped to listen: a deep rumbling, closer than before. She slowed her pace, the others following in silence. From time to time the rumble came again and bit by bit turned into a roar; not a continuous, even sound, like the thunder of a waterfall or of great waves breaking on to the shore, but the savage, unpredictable snarl of some wild beast that has caught the scent of its prey.

Gradually, she noticed the smell. A horrible, rotting, stomach-churning smell, worse than anything she'd experienced before, worse than the Harpies even, and growing stronger all the time. She clutched her mouth.

'Ugh!' cried Florence, coughing, 'I can't take this much longer, we've *got* to find the way out, I can't breathe – '

'Wait,' said Ante, 'I think we're coming to a cave.'

The tunnel widened into a much larger space where the air, while it could hardly be called fresh, felt a bit clearer. The bough illuminated an area about the size of a large room, with a ceiling so high the light couldn't reach it. Three patches of darkness round the walls indicated that they weren't yet out of the maze.

'Phew, this is better,' panted Gil. 'The smell's not so bad in – ouch!'

'What is it?' asked Florence.

Crouching down he rubbed his shin. 'I tripped over something. This.'

Ante turned to cast light on what Gil held in his hand. An object about thirty centimetres long, smooth and pale white.

'It's a bone,' said Florence, 'but a pretty big one. How did that get here?'

'There are more,' said Gil, 'look.'

Shadows criss-crossed each other as Ante waved the bough over shapes scattered on the ground; some long, some curved, or dome-shaped with large round sockets and lines of grinning teeth…

Florence screamed. 'Drop it, Gil! They're *human* bones!'

CHAPTER EIGHTEEN

The Labyrinth

Gil dropped it at once. Florence clapped both hands to her mouth.

Ante shrank back, sickness rising from her stomach, clutching the bough to her body lest it reveal more. Yet not to see what they might tread on would be worse.

Gil scrambled to his feet. 'Those butterflies – Ante, throw some light on the wall.'

They were there again, scattered all over the surface. Sometimes large, standing on its own, or in groups of several smaller ones together, the same design repeated itself: the spread-open wings of a butterfly reduced to simple, symmetrical triangles carved in the stone, divided by a straight line for the head and body, ending in a long tail.

Gil let out a groan. 'No, oh no, they're not butterflies. How could I have been so *slow*? Those aren't wings, they're blades. And the line is the handle – they're double axes.'

Florence looked blank.

'Don't you know what that means? The Double Axe!

This isn't a maze, it's a labyrinth. *The* labyrinth.'

'*The* labyrinth?' echoed Ante.

'Yes, yes, look, I know about this from my father. He's mad about archaeology and he's got a whole box of newspaper clippings about this fellow in Crete who's just discovered the remains of the palace of King Minos, and there is a *real* labyrinth built into the palace with all these Double Axes scratched on to the walls – I can't remember why, something to do with labyrinth coming from the Greek word for axe – and they've found wall paintings and all kinds of artefacts. You must have heard about it – he's digging up new things all the time.'

Digging up – what was he on about? Ante's forehead ached with the effort of working it out. From beside her came a sharp intake of breath.

Florence stood rigid, staring at Gil. 'Are you saying what I think you're saying?' she whispered. 'That the bones – the noise – and that *smell* – oh no, I'm out of here.'

His arm shot out and grabbed her. 'Where to, Florence? Back to the Furies? If there's a Minotaur we'll have to face it, we have no choice – '

'Minotaur?' cried Ante. 'You mean that horrible half-bull thing that ate people? You think it's *here*?'

Gil was too busy struggling with Florence to reply. 'Don't be stupid,' he panted. 'How will you find your way back through the labyrinth on your own? We have to stay togeth – '

He broke off as a roar, louder than any before, filled

the cave. Ante fought back a scream. Florence turned on Gil, her blonde hair tangled around her face, the sleeves of her school blouse crumpled.

'You think *I'm* stupid,' she cried, 'What about you? You're not Theseus. We can't take on the Minotaur! We've got no weapon, *nothing* – '

'We've got the bough,' Ante tried to reply, but her voice was lost as another roar shook the cave. Swivelling round, her eyes darted from the mouth of one tunnel to another so that the patches of darkness jerked and slid together into one blurred whole. Which one? *Which one?*

'We haven't got much time,' said Gil, speaking very fast. 'We must use whatever weapons we have – '

' – which is none – '

' – Shut up, Florence! All right, so what if we haven't got a sword, or Ariadne's thread, we've got to defend ourselves some– '

'We have got thread,' said Ante. 'Penelope's.' Taking the silver-grey ball from her pocket, she held it up, letting it unravel a little.

Gil shook his head. 'No good,' he groaned. 'Theseus only used Ariadne's thread for finding his way out of the labyrinth, not for defeating the Minotaur. It won't help.'

A silver gleam spun through the dark as Florence seized the loose end and wound it round her fingers. 'We must be able to do something with it,' she said. 'It's unbreakable. We could tie the Minotaur up.'

'Oh yes,' said Gil witheringly, 'and first of all we could ask him very politely to lie down so – '

A deafening roar cut him off. The whole cavern reverberated; to Ante it was as if her ribcage were being torn apart from inside. Clutching her hands to her chest she felt the thread grow taut and an idea flashed across her mind. She sprang back, letting the thread unroll, praying that Florence could read her lips because the terrible sound crashing around them drowned all speech. 'We could trip him up!'

Florence dropped to the floor. Two tunnels gaped near each other; Ante crouched down some way apart so that the thread could cover both. That only left the third tunnel, in the wall on the other side of the cave…

Luck was not on their side. The sudden turn of Florence's head, the look of terror in her eyes and Ante swung round on her heels. Her heart seemed to explode in her chest. A huge shape towered over her, a bull's head on a massive neck tossed from side to side, light catching the tips of its long, curved horns and the glitter of hunger in its bloodshot eyes. Human skin, streaked with sweat and filth, rippled over its rib cage and down its abdomen; from the chest up, the skin flowed into black animal hair, stretched over bulging shoulder muscles from which two huge hooves reared up just above her head.

Hooves that could smash a skull as if it were icing sugar.

A scream erupted inside her, tearing through her

throat. She gripped her end of the thread until it cut her flesh. *As if it could be any help now!*

A flash of movement from her left. Head down, Gil hurled himself at the creature's legs. A roar yanked open the muzzle; its sharp, crooked teeth gleamed dully, saliva frothing from its black lips, its head jerked back. For a second the top-heavy torso swayed, hooves flailing the air; then Ante leapt away as it came crashing down. Air rushed past her face, sending something flying from her hand. Then – darkness. She could see nothing. Only the sound on her left – something between a groan and a deep, gasping for air – told her where Gil lay. And Florence –

'We need light, Ante,' came her voice from close by.

Light. Of course. She moved her hand, surprised to find something round locked tightly within her fingers, ah yes, the ball of silver thread. But there should be something else, not circular but long and supple…

Then she realised. 'The bough – it's gone!'

'What?'

'The Minotaur knocked it out of my hand!'

'So it's got to be here somewhere.' From where Florence sat came the sound of scrabbling over the floor.

'Then why can't we see it? Ugh.' Ante's hand brushed against a soft surface, hairy and slimy; she snatched it away at the memory of the slavering mouth and black lips drawn back to bite.

'Look.' Gil had got his breath back at last. 'Never

mind the bough. My rugby tackling skills may still be strong after all these years but I can't hold on to this monster's legs for much longer. What happened to your brilliant idea of tying him up, Florence?'

'But we can't see!'

'No, but you can *feel* him right enough, can't you? Come on, knot the thread round his hoof and through his mouth or something. He must have knocked himself out against the wall when I brought him down but he could come to any minute.'

Ante felt Florence pull on her end of the thread and, with cries of disgust, begin to fumble in the darkness between them.

After a moment came a scraping of shoes on stone and, from above Ante's head, a huge letting out of breath. 'I can't stand this,' gasped Florence. 'I must get some air! That tunnel there – it doesn't look as dark as the others.'

'Florence – no – hang on!' Seizing the thread, Ante felt for the Minotaur's horns to wind it round. Teeth clenched, she tucked it under the matted hair of the leg just above the hoof and pulled it tight before passing it down to Gil to finish off. 'We'll come – just let's find the bough first.'

'I've got to *breathe*!'

'Me too,' panted Gil. 'But we have to work this out. Now, if it were anywhere on the ground, we'd see it. Unless – '

'Oh, no,' said Ante.

'I'm afraid so,' he sighed. 'It's under him. Ante, you and I are the strongest. When I say go, we'll push him over as far as we can and Florence, you'll have to come round and slide your hand under. All right, Florence?'

No reply.

'She hasn't actually gone down that tunnel, has she?' he groaned. 'Florence!'

An answering shout came from not far away, muffled by the echoing walls.

'Looks like it,' said Ante.

'Will she *never* learn?' cried Gil. 'Oh, to hell with her. Can you push with one hand and reach for the bough with the other?'

Push? It was hard enough having to handle the stinking monster to tie it up. But Gil was already straining to take the greater part of its weight, so she held her breath and squeezed her hand under its filthy belly. Her fingers closed on the familiar shape and in a moment the warm light filled the cave once more, falling on a face at the mouth of the tunnel to the left of the Minotaur's head. 'Florence!' Ante cried, 'Where've you been?'

The blue eyes shone with excitement. 'I've found the way out! I thought I could see light and I was right. Follow me!' She disappeared, feeling her way swiftly along the wall.

Ante groaned. Florence had to be the leader, no matter what. She scrambled to her feet to follow.

'Wait.' Gil didn't move. He stared up at the wall above

the tunnel to the right of the Minotaur's head. 'Ante, bring the bough here. Quickly.'

'Not more butterflies – axes – we know what they're for,' she sighed. 'You told us.'

'*Quickly.*'

Leaning over the Minotaur's body, she held the bough up high. Light fell on lines scratched into the rock. 'There's something written over the tunnel. D – E, no, A – E – '

'It's not all there,' he said. 'Look, there's another D, but next to it just a line. The rest of the letter's worn away.'

'Well, it looks to me as if it's trying to spell DEAD,' said Ante. 'So I'm glad Florence didn't go down there. Maybe there's a message above all of them – hey, what's the matter?'

Gil was staring at her, thunderstruck. The next minute he leaped forward and snatched the bough from her hand.

'*Gil!*'

On the far side of the cave shadows danced where he waved the bough all round the third tunnel. 'You're right, Ante. There's something written here too. A – S – I – P – H.'

'Asiph? As if? It's rubbish, Gil.'

She stepped back as he sprang to her side, his gaze now fixed on the rock above the first tunnel, the one down which Florence had gone only moments before.

'C – A – R – U,' Ante spelt out. 'The rest is too faded.

Come on, Gil, it probably doesn't mean anything. Let's go.'

For a second Gil stared up at the rock, light from the bough deepening the shadows in his frown of concentration. Then his eyes widened. 'Oh no.'

Ante held out her arm. 'The b – '

'Florence!' he yelled. 'Stop!' The corner of his jacket glanced off Ante's fingernails as he shot past her down the tunnel.

Ante gazed after him. What was going on? Had they both gone crazy? Gil snatching the bough, leaving her in total darkness! With a sigh she straightened up. No choice but to follow. As for Gil – just wait till she caught up with him.

CHAPTER NINETEEN

The Fall of Icarus

Almost at once she saw what Florence meant. The darkness here was thinner. Twenty steps down, she let her hands fall, no longer needing to cling to the rock for guidance. A cold, grey light outlined Gil's figure some way ahead and proved Florence's discovery: this passage led into the open.

It was only later she realised that was all the light guiding Gil too. The bough gave out none at all.

Why were they hurtling along like this, her hands smarting from the grazing from the rock wall and her feet sliding on loose stones? No use begging Gil to slow down and explain, he seemed to have forgotten her altogether as he sped after Florence, calling her name.

At last came an answering cry, only a little way ahead. 'I can see the opening! Nearly th– '

'*No!*' With a spurt of energy Gil disappeared round a corner. Ante, following, blinked as the tunnel broadened into a clear, straight path, filled with white light that poured in through the mouth at the end. For a split second a slight figure ran towards the light; then a scream burst through the air as Gil hurled himself on Florence, bringing her to the ground in a whirl of arms and legs, dust and scattered stones.

Ante stopped still. Gil could have no idea what he was in for. She waited a few moments to catch her breath and then, taking as long as she could, walked towards the struggling pair.

Gil had Florence pinned to the ground with one arm while with the other he tried to ward off a rain of vicious kicks and blows.

'*What – is – WITH – you, Gil?*' Florence yelled. 'Have you gone *completely mad?*'

'Just let me explain – '

'Are you so pleased with your *amazing* rugby tackle on the Minotaur that you just have to try it on everyone else too?'

Gil, already flushed with effort, turned an even deeper red. He hardly noticed when Ante stepped forward and took the bough from his hand.

'Listen, you vicious little cat,' he said through clenched teeth, 'I couldn't make you stop any other way. If you'll just stop fighting – *stop* – for one minute, I'll explain.'

Florence glared from Gil to Ante. The tension went out of her and Gil released his hold. She sat up, trying to smooth down her crumpled clothes before wiping a hand across her cheek, where the long, red scratch left by Cerberus had opened again.

Gil blinked. 'I'm sorry I hurt you. Are – are you all right?'

He was rewarded with a look of withering contempt. 'I thought you were going to explain things to me,' she said. 'Well go on. I'm listening.'

He nodded, got up and, one eye resting on Florence as if afraid she might make a break for it again, crept the short distance to the tunnel opening.

Ante and Florence watched, puzzled, as, with a soft cry, he turned and stumbled back towards them.

'What – ' began Florence.

'It's what I feared.' He sat down heavily next to them. 'The path isn't there.'

'Isn't *there?*'

'Just a straight drop. Straight down. I couldn't see the bottom.'

Florence stared from him to the opening and back again. 'You mean – I would've gone over! I would have, too. I – I didn't think.'

There was a silence.

'I've been stupid,' said Florence at last. 'Really, really *stupid*. And I thought, this time, it was so clearly the way to go and you two were just being slow on the uptake – ' She broke off and stared down at the ground, her face reddening. Blinking several times, she mumbled: 'Sorry, Gil.'

To her surprise, Ante felt a stab of sympathy. Finding herself in the wrong once must be hard enough; but *twice* – hardly an experience Florence was used to. She glanced at Gil.

But he wasn't listening. Hands clasped around his

knees, he rocked back and forth, gazing over their heads at something only he could see. His lips moved, but he spoke so softly Ante had to bend close to hear. 'Will it do? Will it be enough?'

'Will what do?'

He turned to her with a look of such bleakness, such utter hopelessness that she was alarmed. 'Will it work, do you think? I stopped her going over – '

'I know,' put in Florence. 'Thank you.'

' – I stopped her.' His eyes searched Ante's face. 'But will it be enough?'

Understanding dawned on Ante and the colour flooded into her cheeks.

So. He'd guessed.

Guessed what had really happened on the organ loft. That the crash and sound of splintering wood had claimed its victim and that, back in the real world, Florence's body lay, still as stone, on the assembly hall floor, just as Gil's had done, a hundred years before. Did he think that by saving Florence from a terrible fall here, down in Hades, he could somehow undo that fatal event, bring her back to life? *He cares that much about her*, she thought with a pang. *Even now.*

Then she began to tremble as a new thought struck her.

He was trying to save *her*.

For if Florence was dead, then she, Ante, was the cause. Is that what he suspected? A memory flashed across her brain: the three of them collapsed on the ground, panting in the heat from the River of Flame, Gil turning to her suddenly, a new look in his eye... *It's yours, the bough, not Florence's. That – changes things.* Oh god, was that it? The reason she, and she alone, had been able to pluck the bough and guide them all through Hades: *because she was the only one still alive?*

The eyes fixed on hers seemed to scorch her soul. She looked away. Broken rock and stony ground blurred into one grey mass.

Florence leapt into the gap. 'Of *course* it's enough, Gil. What do you mean? You stopped me going over the edge. That's enough for me.'

The faintest movement. Beside her Ante sensed Gil lift his gaze from her to focus it on Florence.

'But what I want to know,' Florence went on, 'is how you *knew* – '

Here it comes. Ante dug her fingernails into the palms of her hands.

' – that the passage would end like that, in a sheer drop. Or was it just a hunch?'

Ante's fingers uncurled.

'The – the letters. Over the mouth of the tunnel,' stammered Gil. 'There were different letters over each one.'

Florence shrugged. 'So? What do a few random letters matter?'

She was back to herself again. Strange how reassuring this felt.

'They weren't random. They were names, partly

worn away, which is why I didn't recognise them at first.' His voice was steadier now. 'It was D-A-E-D that gave me the clue. Ante thought it looked like DEAD, which it did, but then I realised it could be the first half of Daedalus. After that it was easy. C-A-R-U clearly should read Icarus and A-S-I-P-H should read Pasiphae.'

'Clearly,' remarked Florence.

Ante was relieved to find she wasn't the only one to have no idea what Gil was talking about.

'Go on, then,' urged Florence.

'Well, isn't it obvious?' Gil cried. 'Daedalus and Icarus, remember?' He looked from one to the other. 'Don't you know anything? What *do* you learn at school nowadays?'

This couldn't go unchallenged.

'We know quite a lot, actually,' said Florence, 'probably a lot more stuff than you. History, Geography, Chemistry, Physics, Biology – just because we don't waste our time learning a whole lot of dead languages and old stories that are no use to anyone anymore – '

'Anyway,' broke in Ante, equally stung, 'I thought you said you were rubbish at Latin and Greek and all that stuff. How come you're such a geek after all?'

'A *what*?'

'A nerd, an anorak, a boffin – a – oh, you know what I mean.'

'No,' he said shortly, 'I don't.'

'She means you're a – oh what does my mum call it?'

said Florence. 'Oh yes. A swot. Because you seem to know everything,' she added hastily, as his face darkened.

'I am not a swot. Or a geek, or whatever you call it. I *am* lousy at Latin and Greek. The only thing that's bearable about the lessons is the stories, which everybody knows anyway.'

'We don't,' said Florence. 'Oh all right, some of them. Theseus and the Minotaur, for instance.'

'Except that you don't seem to know why there was a Minotaur in the first place. It was the result of King Minos's wife, Pasiphae, falling in love with a bull – the Minotaur was their child, you see – I know, I know, but this kind of thing goes on in myths all the time. So King Minos ordered Daedalus, who was this really clever inventor, to build the labyrinth to imprison the Minotaur. Then Daedalus wanted to leave Crete, but the king wouldn't let him, he was far too useful, you see, so he made wings for himself and his son, Icarus, out of birds' feathers and fixed them on with wax. That meant they could fly away from Crete and escape. But Icarus flew too near the sun, the wax melted, his wings fell off and he plunged to his death in the sea.'

Gil paused for a moment.

'So when I worked out what the letters stood for, it struck me that the one tunnel we *shouldn't* take, the one tunnel that could only lead to disaster, was the one named after Icarus. And that,' he looked at Florence, 'was the one you took.'

A silence fell.

'You realise what this means,' said Florence after a moment.

'Oh no,' groaned Ante.

'I'm afraid so,' sighed Gil. 'We have to go back to the Minotaur and pick one of the other tunnels. But which one?'

'What happened to Daedalus?' asked Florence. 'Did he get away safely?'

Gil nodded.

'Then that's the tunnel we'll take. Come on.' Rising to her feet, Florence wavered, an uncertain look in her eye. 'At least, if you think – if you both think – that's a good idea?'

'Sure,' mumbled Ante, surprised.

But Gil grinned. 'Sounds good to me,' he said. 'You don't always get it wrong, Florence. Just most of the time.'

'Great. Thanks.'

Hiding a smile, Ante led the way back up the tunnel. Ten paces from the end, her heart jumped into her throat as a groan tore through the air; a long animal cry of pain and bewilderment, rising to a bellow of rage. Light jerked up the walls. Gripping the bough to steady it, she forced her footsteps into the cave.

CHAPTER TWENTY

Shadows Under the Ice

It would have been a comical sight, a pitiful one even, if it hadn't been so terrifying.

The Minotaur squirmed on the ground, trying to get to his feet, thwarted by the way his hooves refused to detach themselves from his horns. Holding her breath, Ante tiptoed past, Gil and Florence following. Thick muscles stood out on the bull neck as he strove to turn enough to lunge with his horns; his huge eyes rolled, bulging with effort, and froze. They'd fallen on the bough in Ante's hand.

He stopped mid-roar. Waves of sound crashing over their heads ceased. But the moment Ante got the three of them past and into the second tunnel, he came to life once more, his snarls of rage pursuing them as they descended. When at last they died away, a silence fell that no one had the will to break.

Deeper and deeper into the gloom the passage took them. It didn't look as though the tunnel would ever bring them out on to the path down the gorge; indeed, it dawned on Ante that this *was* now the path and for all they knew, they could be following this steep, winding tunnel forever. From a glance back, it looked as if the same idea had occurred to the others. Gil walked head bent, grey eyes fixed unblinking on some point on the ground in front of him. Florence plodded a few paces behind, shoulders sagging, arms hanging by her sides, as if every step into darkness sucked a little more life out of her.

A little more life... At the back of Ante's mind a floodgate opened. All those fears she'd tried to suppress, the ones chased away by the immediate danger of the Minotaur, rushed through, shooting up and spilling over into every corner of her brain.

Florence was dead.

She, Ante, had killed her.

By standing back and watching Florence walk into danger, Ante had engineered her death. That was why the ilex had withheld its bough not just from Gil, but from Florence too. *Neither of them would be going back.*

Then a wild hope struck her. If Florence was dead, why did that filthy old ferryman refuse to take her over the Styx? Why didn't she have a coin like Gil did? Her heart lifted at the thought that Gil must've got it wrong, that Florence was still alive, that the fall had never happened!

Unless...

'Hey, what's the matter, Ante?' said Gil.

She'd stopped so suddenly he'd stumbled into her, Florence close at his heels.

'N-nothing,' she stammered, without looking round. 'Nothing. Sorry.'

Clenching her teeth to concentrate on the path ahead, she tried with all her strength to banish the question now taking shape in her mind.

What if Florence had fallen over, but hadn't died at once? What if, at the beginning of this strange journey, her body had been lying, dying slowly, on the floor of the assembly hall?

A shudder went through her. Light danced over the uneven rock.

From behind came Gil's calm, steady voice. 'Stop for a moment.'

'Are you all right, Ante?' said Florence. 'We can stop if you need a rest.'

She felt a hand touch her arm with a gentleness that cut her to the quick. *No! Not now! Don't be nice to me, not now I know what I've done!*

'I'm fine,' she gulped, not daring to turn round.

'Well I'm not surprised you're shivering,' said Florence, dropping her arm and tugging at the sleeves of her sweatshirt, tied around her waist. 'Have you noticed how cold it's getting?'

It was true. With Phlegethon behind them, intense heat had changed gradually to warmth, then to a slight coolness and now, as the passage led them further and further down, a chill sharpened the air. Florence pulled her sweatshirt over her head, readjusting the strap of her waterskin as she did so, and Gil buttoned up his jacket as high as he could.

Fingers trembling, Ante undid her own jumper from round her and thrust it back on. 'We'd better keep moving,' she muttered, 'and hope it starts getting warmer again.'

It didn't. The cold came creeping towards them. For a while no one spoke, their minds taken up with the simple task of keeping warm. Ante pulled her sleeve down over the hand that held the bough, willing the cold to numb her thoughts as effectively as it numbed her fingers and toes.

After a while the passage became less steep and the darkness grew thinner. A draught tugged at her hair and clothes, increasing as the light grew stronger but somehow never brighter, until turning a sharp corner, she came to a stop.

Anything, she'd thought, anything would be better than to be walking forever in darkness, trapped in that endless tunnel of cold stone. But relief at having at last reached its mouth was quickly crushed by the desolation that met her eyes.

The path had vanished. Before her stretched a frozen landscape, pale and grey in the dim light, flat as a lake of ice except where flurries of snow had been whipped into drifts. On either side, the rocky gorge rose starkly before disappearing into gloom. As she peered outwards, the wind snatched the hair off her face and blew down her neck. Her eyes watered.

Florence fell back into the shelter of the tunnel, hugging herself against the cold. 'What now?' she hissed through clenched teeth.

'We seem to've reached the bottom,' said Gil. 'So this must be it, I suppose. Where I'm – I'm meant to be.' His brow furrowed as he glanced around the grey-white expanse.

'But there's nothing here!' cried Florence. 'What are you supposed to do? What are *we* – ' she stopped. Folding her arms, she leaned back against the wall and pursed her lips.

Nothing there… Ante bent into the wind, screwing her eyes to slits. Keeping the bough low – in such vastness its glow softened details, making them less distinct – she strained to make out… *yes*. A low roofline, about a hundred metres away, only a glimpse before a swirl of snow blotted it out; but that was enough. 'There is something,' she murmured. 'Over there. Come on.'

The wind screamed in her ears, blocking out all other sound. Snow stung her cheeks as she stepped across the ice, her feet tense with the effort to stop them from sliding under her. In the lull between blasts of wind she could hear Gil and Florence gasping as they stumbled behind, and above that… a strange, mournful music, like the cries of a thousand seagulls, rolling in waves over the frozen landscape. She scanned the distance for sight of the birds, the curve of their wings dotting the space above them. Nothing.

Then a dark shape appeared in the ice near her feet.

That was new. Her eye caught another, not far away, and another – suddenly they lay everywhere. Debris trapped as the lake froze, presumably. Between them the way lay clear in a straight, narrow line, almost like a causeway; she began to pick her way along this.

Dark, uneven shapes, some far, far below, some near the surface…

Florence screamed. Ante's eyes flew to where she stood rigid, gaze fixed in horror at a spot near her feet. And from under the ice a face stared back at her, its bared white teeth gleaming against livid skin and tendrils of rough, black hair.

CHAPTER TWENTY-ONE

The Control Room

The ice slid under Ante, wrenching her knees, but she didn't slow down. Her heart pounded. Ahead she could just make out a few lines in the mist – the angle of a low roof, the corner of a building – before snatching her eyes back to the ground, lest she should trip, oh god, *fall* on a solid patch of darkness. Her stomach rose; clutching it with one arm she fought with the other to keep her balance.

Out of the mist loomed a door. Her breath rushed out in a cry as she grasped the handle and turned it with all her strength. The door opened and she fell through, Gil and Florence panting behind.

'Well, well, well. What a miserable lot you are.'

Ante blinked. Yellow light bulbs hanging from the ceiling lit up a narrow, windowless room. Half-way along one wall a fire burnt in the grate, giving welcome warmth to her limbs, stiff with cold. To the left of the fireplace she could just make out the lines of a closed door. Behind her an icy draught blew from the way she'd come in, hitting the backs of her knees and scattering snowflakes across the wooden floor.

The bright light hurt her eyes but she didn't dare close them. Because then she saw again that hideous figure, suspended forever in ice, whose eyes were colder than stone. Not with death. They had moved and followed her as she shrank away, and the blackened lips seemed to be trying to speak. A kind of living death.

'Shut the door, one of you! Were you born in a barn?'

She looked round but Gil was quicker. The blast of wind and snow from the open door ceased. Turning back, she focussed on the source of the cool, half-mocking voice, the blur of shapes and tones in the room sharpening into outlines as her eyes got used to the glare.

At the far end stood a heavy, wooden desk, littered with documents and maps. A pair of binoculars, a glass and a half-empty bottle of wine jostled for space among all the papers. Reclining in his chair sat a slim, thin-lipped man in military uniform, wearing dark glasses and an enormous smile. His arms were folded and his long legs, crossed at the ankles, rested on the edge of the desk, where the wine bottle and glass seemed in imminent danger of being swept off by his gleaming leather boots.

'Antonia, Virgil and Florence.' The man drawled the names, as if savouring each one. 'What a pleasure, what a very great pleasure to meet you at last.'

Ante flinched. Something about this smooth, lazy, yet powerful tone was familiar. Behind the dark glasses the man seemed to be looking at once at all of them and at her alone.

'And I've taken enormous interest in your progress. You really have done awfully well, you know. Take a look, if you like.'

He waved at the lines of small screens – ten, twenty, thirty, Ante lost count – arranged on the walls around his desk. Many showed a dark, bare cliff with a path jutting out from it. On some of the screens tiny figures walked downwards. Others showed sections of a pedestrianised shopping area dotted with stalls; large, clumsy figures wandered aimlessly from one stall to another.

'Security cameras,' said Florence in a dazed voice.

Gil stared from one screen to another, open-mouthed. 'Photographs – but they're *moving*! Look!'

'Don't get too excited,' Ante sighed.

But Gil brushed past her and made straight for the wall on the far side of the desk, oblivious of the long-legged man, who swivelled in his chair to watch his progress with open amusement. Darting from screen to screen, he hardly gave himself time to register one before moving on to the next. 'That's the Styx – and there's Charon – he must be rowing back, his boat's empty – and there's where the path begins – '

He started and turned pale. Ante snatched a glance at the screen he'd just reached; enough to make out the dark, cell-like room, the crimson glow of fires and the black, hooded shapes crawling across the floor.

'Ah yes, the Fortress of Dis.' The man lingered caressingly over each word. 'One of my favourite places. Not that I don't find the Multivice Complex satisfying in its own way.' Stretching out his body, he rested the back of his head on his hands and gazed at the ceiling. 'Sins of the Flesh have their own special charm. Gorgeous Gluttony, Chilled-out Sloth – '

Something chimed in Ante's brain. 'So it was you! The voice – "Hades-is-us, the Shopping Maul!"' She whirled round to Florence and Gil. 'Don't you remember?'

Florence's brow cleared. 'Of course. "Awesome Anger, Something-or-other Envy – "'

The man beamed. 'So you liked my Introduction, eh? And what do you think of it all?'

'Wh – what do we think of what?' said Ante.

'The Shopping Maul, of course. The Multivice Complex. Isn't it brilliant?'

'Well – '

'And the best of it all is, you gave me the idea! My top designers would never have come up with a place as ghastly as that.'

She gaped at him. '*I did*?'

'No, no, not you personally of course, must you be so literal? Your species. I never cease to be amazed by the bursting creativity of the human race. The way you

160

take rather dull little bits of countryside and transform them into magnificent concrete shopping malls and vast, popcorn-studded cinema complexes. So deliciously practical for covering more than one vice, too, what with greed, avarice, envy, pride, sloth – and lust and anger are always easy to fit in.'

Gil looked helplessly at Ante and Florence. The man gave them no chance to explain. 'Do tell me what you think,' he continued. 'Customer feedback is so important. Then we can incorporate public reaction into any new design.'

Ante chewed her lip, trying to make sense of this. From their expressions, Gil and Florence were grappling with it too.

'Let's get this straight,' said Florence after a moment. 'We've come on a long journey through some horrible places – the Shopping Maul, the Fortress of Dis, the labyrinth – '

'The labyrinth!' The man's mood of easy languor vanished. He jumped to his feet and in two strides reached one of the screens behind the desk. Examining it carefully, a frown creasing his smooth forehead, he took a mobile from his pocket. 'Persephone? Find Gordius, would you and put him on. Thanks.'

Gil, fascinated, stared at him.

'Gordius? Got a job for you. Labyrinth, sector 2578… Yes… Yes, him…Well, he seems to have got himself a bit tied up… No, I wouldn't be bothering you if we could cut the thread, would I? It's been dipped in the Styx... Well, you do have a way with knots... Do what you can. Thanks.' He slipped the phone back in his pocket and, sighing heavily, turned back to his desk. 'Troublesome lot, aren't you?'

On the screen behind him, an infra-red camera showed something huge and only partly human writhing on a stony floor. From time to time it raised its savage bull's head and bared its teeth in a silent roar.

'But it was attacking us!' protested Ante.

'So? That's the kind of thing you have to expect down here. This isn't a holiday camp, you know.'

'When you say *down here*,' said Florence, 'do you mean we're in – we're in – that this is – '

'Hell?' The man said softly. 'Yes.'

Ante froze. The word tolled in her head with a slow, dreamlike horror. *Hell...Hell...we're in Hell.* 'But – the ticket-collector – Fabian – called it Hades,' she stammered. 'The – the Underworld, Kingdom of the Dead. Not Hell.'

'They are all the same place.' The man's voice was even gentler than before. 'For some it is more Hellish than for others. Those bores in Elysium, for instance – they might just as well not be here. But most customers find it – rather different.'

'So if this is Hell,' whispered Florence, 'then – *who are you?*'

The man smiled. 'Can't you guess?' Leaning back

in his chair, he put his fingertips together and swivelled round playfully towards each of them in turn.

His smile broadened. 'Yes, I thought you could,' he murmured.

CHAPTER TWENTY-TWO

The Designs of Evil

Ante was the first to speak. 'The Devil.' Her voice came out dry and cracked. 'You're the Devil.' She felt she was going to choke.

He frowned. 'You know, I really, really don't like that name.' He paused to suck air through his teeth. 'It has all sorts of unfortunate connotations. People dressing up in silly costumes and jabbering on and on about Dark Forces. Or they imagine that I go round 'tempting' them to steal cars or fiddle their tax returns or cheat on their partner. As if I had the time.' He gave a deep sigh. 'The fact is, people don't need my help to get down here. They do it on their own. I just run the place. Every person who comes has their own special niche in one of the Circles, from the Multivice Complex near the top to Cocytus at the very bottom, where we are now. We never turn anyone away. And the further down you go, the more rewarding it becomes.'

'Wh – what do you mean, "rewarding"?' ventured Ante.

'Well haven't you seen? I'm not talking about a bunch

of Harpies spoiling all the fun for a few gluttons: I mean real, calculating, cold-blooded criminals. The Fortress of Dis specialises in liars and thieves' – he shot a sidelong glance at Florence, who blushed and looked down – 'what do you think comes below them? Armed robbers? Yes. Kidnappers, terrorists? Them too. And murderers.'

'Are you OK, Ante?' said Florence. 'You look pale as a ghost.'

'I – I'm OK,' stammered Ante. That word, anything but that! She pushed it to the back of her mind. 'I – was just thinking – those faces – '

The Devil smiled. 'Ah yes, them,' he said. 'So you do look about you. I thought as much. The faces under the ice. Now I think they really are my favourites.'

'Wh – who are they?'

'There are different degrees even in murder, you know.'

Did she imagine it, or was he speaking to her alone? Behind the dark glasses it was difficult to tell.

'There are those who do away with just one or two people to get what they want. Their hearts are cold but they still have some traces of humanity. They lie at the top of the ice and never cease to moan.'

The cries of seagulls, Ante remembered. Not seagulls, then.

'After that you have an altogether more sophisticated type who have raised murder and betrayal to an art form – Livia, Caligula, Nero, Cesare Borgia, your very own

Richard the Third of England – they're all there, a little lower down, of course. Thousands of them. They're still vaguely recognisable but I'm glad to say they make no sound at all, what with their tears being frozen and their mouths burnt away. And finally, you have the *real* masters of their art.'

Leaning back in his chair, he gave a satisfied sigh.

'Yes,' he continued dreamily, gazing beyond his audience into a world only he could see. 'The genocides. The mass murderers. Their souls are ice long before they reach me. Do you know, I have some down there that are responsible for the murders of *millions* of people.'

'Hitler,' said Florence in a flat voice. 'And Stalin.'

'Among others. The twentieth century produced a particularly fine crop, I'm proud to say, with quite a few more still to come. I'm looking forward to meeting them.'

'So the – the faces we passed,' faltered Ante, 'they could've been among them?'

'Oh no, they'll have no human form left at all. They are imprisoned deep down in the very heart of Cocytus, where the ice is colder than you can understand, and every scrap of flesh has been flayed from their bones.'

A silence fell.

Then Gil spoke. 'I don't understand. All right, so we've somehow reached the bottom of Hell. But what I want to know is: *why are we here?*'

'Why indeed? Why would three perfectly innocent

school children be condemned to the depths of Hell? Where traitors and murderers are punished? You tell me.'

This is it, thought Ante. *Now they'll know for certain.* She stared down at the floor. *Don't let them look at me. Don't let them see –*

No danger of that. Mastering her trembling, she stole a glance at her companions. Their eyes were fixed on the Devil as he drew out his meaning with tantalising slowness. *Cat and mouse,* she thought suddenly.

'Do you know what lies beyond that door?' He indicated with a slight movement of his head the door by the fireplace. 'It's a big place, Cocytus. Some who come here aren't so easy to define. They've committed a terrible crime but they aren't – how shall I put it – really *sold* on the idea. So hard for them to move on when they're still just going over and over the same old thing. They remain stuck in their world and they bring it with them.'

Ante felt the blood rise to her cheeks. Now, *now* they must all be staring at her, they must *know*…but then she caught sight of Gil's face, pale and shaken, and his eyes, focussed not on her but on some invisible spot straight before him.

Only Florence, frowning, returned the Devil's gaze. 'What do you mean?'

'But *what* a world!' he continued, ignoring her. 'You know, I really do have to hand it to you and your kind for showing me a thing or two. Here am I, for thousands of years Chief Designer of Instruments of Torment and Suffering, by which souls are torn apart by wild beasts, or burnt perpetually in raging fires, or boiled in rivers of blood, or frozen in ice – but in terms of creating the perfect Hell – well, you humans showed me the way in 1914.'

He got to his feet, walked round the desk and stood in front of them. Firelight gleamed on his brass buttons and belt buckle. Reaching beside him, he picked up a peaked cap made, like the rest of his uniform, from a thick, khaki material, and tapped it softly on the side of his leg.

Ante gasped. It was only the colour she hadn't recognised. He should have been in black and white, like the photographs in her history book. 'You're a soldier,' she said. 'Are – are you an officer?'

He smiled. 'You could say that. I am Commander-in-Chief, All Armies, circa 1917, as Gil here would know very well if – ' he stopped.

Gil looked bewildered. 'Wh – what would I know if *what*?'

'Your future. Or rather, what should have been your future, if that amusing little episode in the organ loft hadn't intervened. As I said, some people get stuck in their world. Didn't you ever wonder, all those hundred years, why you were still there? Long after all your friends had grown up and died and moved on?'

'Of course I did! All the time!'

'Wait a minute,' Florence cut in. 'You said some

murderers get stuck in their own world. What's that got to do with Gil? He hasn't murdered anyone.'

The Devil didn't even give her a glance. 'And what do you think happened to those friends of yours, just a few years later? You can't know, of course, but *they* do. You're studying it in school now, aren't you my dears?' He smiled at Ante and Florence.

Poor Gil, thought Ante suddenly, *he has no idea*. She looked at Florence and saw the alarm in her eye. It was one thing to read about the horrors in history books, with their old black and white photographs of appalling suffering that happened long, long ago; it was quite another to relive it with someone who could have been there and whose friends certainly were.

'They don't want to tell you,' mocked the Devil. 'Touching, isn't it? No hurry, girls, just take your time.'

He leaned back against the desk and folded his arms. Gil's eyes darted eagerly from one face to another.

Cat and mouse. A surge of anger went through Ante and for a moment she couldn't trust herself to speak.

It was Florence who answered. 'The Great War. 1914 to 1918.'

Gil's eyes lit up. 'A war!' he cried. 'And I missed it! I can't believe – '

'No!' Ante was surprised at her own vehemence. 'It wasn't like that. People did think it was, at the beginning, they thought it would be all heroic and stuff. But they just ended up sitting in soaking trenches for years and millions of men got blown up or drowned in the mud. It was terrible.'

'Terrible, terrible,' agreed the Devil. 'But good for you, eh, Gil? You managed to miss it. Smart move, that. Your friends weren't so lucky.'

This was too much for Florence. 'How can you have a go at him for that? It's not his fault he was killed – *murdered* – before he could take part in the war. What about the boy who killed him? He should be down here, not Gil.'

'Ah, yes, him,' replied the Devil thoughtfully. 'I was wondering when we'd come to him. What was his name now, nasty piece of work, wasn't he Gil?'

'Harry.' Gil spoke barely above a whisper. He seemed to have shrunk into himself, staring at the ground with a hopelessness Ante knew only too well.

So the fear could go on then. Even after death.

'Harry. Yes, thought you'd remember. Well, you'll be glad to know he didn't live a lot longer than you.'

He got up and walked in a leisurely fashion round to the front of the desk. Opening a drawer, he took out a large, leather-bound book. Gil, not daring to move a muscle, watched him leaf through the pages.

'Let me see now,' he murmured. 'Ah yes, here he is. Flanders, October 1917. Passchendaele.'

CHAPTER TWENTY-THREE

Exile

No one spoke. For a second everything seemed to dissolve and Ante was back in the classroom, history book open before her, shiny pages showing a sea of mud and craters and blackened trees, broken in places by shattered, twisted limbs protruding from lumps of grey and sodden uniform…

She shuddered. Florence, too, looked shaken. The officer sat down at his desk again and leaned back, hands clasped behind his head, thin lips stretched into a broad smile.

'That's – ' Ante began and stopped. He deserved something, this killer – she flinched as the word set up an unbearable echo in her mind – but *Passchendaele*… Clearing her throat, she tried again. 'The bloodiest battle in the whole war. Hundreds of thousands of men slaughtered.'

'My, my, we do know our history, don't we?' said the Devil. 'As I said, I can only admire the ingenuity of your species. And I am always willing to learn from others.'

'What do you mean?'

'I mean that now you know what lies behind that door. So the only question remaining is – *which of you is destined to go through?*'

He gazed with evident satisfaction at the three faces in front of him, now pale with shock. Ante felt as if her legs were dissolving beneath her.

'Y-you're saying,' she stammered, fighting to control the shaking that had taken over her body, 'that out there you've got a First World War battle going on? Forever? With the same people being gassed and wounded and screaming and dying, *forever*?' Her voice ended in a kind of shriek.

'Put that thing down!'

She jumped. The Devil was no longer smiling. In her distress she'd raised her hands to her face and a golden ray from the bough streamed across his desk. She dropped them immediately.

'Quite the little drama queen, aren't you?' All trace of the light, half-teasing tone had disappeared. The voice was hard and cold. 'I am talking about the model, not the event. When your species hit on the idea of trench warfare in your world, you gave me the perfect inspiration for mine. As for the dead themselves, I have no power over them, except for the ones that come to me. Now, to business.'

He closed the book and returned it to the drawer. Taking his phone out of his pocket, he tapped some buttons and stared at the screen. Beside Ante, Gil stiffened, his eyes glued to the gadget as before.

'As I thought.' The Devil looked up. 'I've checked today's agenda. The three of you arrived as expected, but now your journey together is over. Only one of you goes through that door. As to which one – well, I imagine you'll have worked that out by now.'

Ante looked at Gil and Florence and in their pale faces read the fear that was in her own. She tried to say something but no words came. A cloud seemed to come across her vision and through it the door loomed, towering above her. Dimly she became aware that the Devil was speaking again.

'One of you has a debt to pay. To pay at a high price, the highest of all. Because one of you is a traitor. Or a murderer. Both are punished here, in Cocytus. You may have killed someone directly, in cold blood. Or you may have watched that person walk to their death, which you could have prevented, and chose not to. Perhaps you betrayed the trust of someone weaker than yourself and left him, left all your friends to be slaughtered with thousands of others on a muddy battlefield – '

'You can't *do* that!' cried Florence. 'You can't blame Gil for dying before the war even started. What kind of reasoning is that? Just because he missed out on the battle of Passchendaele you're saying he's got to go and take part in it now?'

'I am not saying anything. I am merely offering suggestions. The lot falls to one of you. I could do the selecting, of course,' he added, smiling broadly. 'But it's far more entertaining to watch you sort it out for yourselves.'

'You psycho!' screamed Florence. 'Suppose we refuse? Suppose none of us goes?' She wheeled round to Ante and Gil. 'Come on, we're not having this. If we stand together he can't – '

'It's all right, Florence.' Ante felt a rushing in her ears. Her voice came out small and thin, as if it wasn't hers but somebody else's, from far away. 'It's me.'

Her words hung in the air like steel wire. It took Florence and Gil a moment to understand; then they rounded on her.

'Don't be silly – '

'It can't be you – '

They saw her face and their words died away.

'I'm the one who betrayed my friend,' said Ante. 'Only you weren't my friend then. You were my worst enemy. You made my life hell from the first day of term.'

Florence reddened, looking down at the floor.

'I thought – I thought because we'd known each other before, at St Dunstan's, it'd be great meeting up again. But I did something to you there, I don't know what. Stole something from you, according to Gil.' She flashed him a glance. 'If you'd just told me, I'd have given it back a hundred times over.'

Florence opened her mouth to speak but closed it again, shaking her head. The flush stealing over her skin deepened.

'It's almost as if you – you preferred just to hate me. My size, my clothes, my trumpet-playing – that especially. For some reason you hated that most of all.'

'Ante, I – I know, I've been horrible.' Florence's head shot up, her gaze seeking hers. 'I'm really – '

'Then I cracked. I lost it completely. And when you came after me, right into the organ loft – I watched your hand move along the – along the broken rail – '

'So you knew it was broken! And you said nothing!'

Ante trembled. She couldn't look at Florence. She stared at the desk, struggling to find words for what she couldn't explain.

'Something stopped me. I – don't know what.' Her voice caught in her throat. 'Fear, panic – ' *No.* She wouldn't get out of it that way. 'Not just that. Part of me – hoped something would happen.'

Now she turned and forced her eyes to meet Florence's. The mix of shock and bewilderment in their expression was agony.

'It was only for a moment!' she pleaded. 'I never thought it would kill you. As soon as I heard the crash I realised something terrible had happened. So when you came running after me down the tunnel I thought, thank God, you hadn't fallen, I hadn't killed you, it was all OK.'

'So where's the problem then?' said Gil, 'She's all right, isn't she?'

'Look,' said Ante wearily. 'One of us is a murderer – or a traitor, whatever you like to call it – how many choices do we have? Not you, Gil, you were the victim of a murderer. Not you, Florence; however nasty you were, you never tried to kill me. That only leaves me.'

She paused. Gil and Florence stood still, eyes fixed on her face.

'I think – I think the crash did kill you, Florence. Not at once. When we all started out you must still've been alive. But only just. You guessed, didn't you Gil, when you saved her in the labyrinth? *Will it be enough*? you asked. Enough to put right the fall she'd already suffered from the organ loft – enough to save me as well as her. I didn't understand at the time but I do now. You've – you've been a good friend.'

The skin around Gil's eyes creased. His mouth twisted as if he badly wanted to say something. Yet he didn't speak.

'So,' finished Ante, 'this is it. I'm the one with the debt to pay, not you. I'm sorry, Florence. If I could change what happened, I would. Here' – she held out the bough – 'take this.'

Light flooded the space between them. Out of the corner of her eye she saw the Devil flinch.

'You carry it now. I – I don't think I should anymore.'

Florence stepped back. 'No!'

'It's all right, it's not theft if I give it to you. You'll both need it if you're ever to get out of here. You're free now.'

Thrusting the bough at her, Ante made a grab for the door handle.

'Ante, wait – '

Wind buffeted through the open doorway. Ante met it full on, letting it fill her ears, drowning Florence's words, and stumbled out.

Behind her, the door slammed shut.

CHAPTER TWENTY-FOUR

The Waste Land

Rain on her face, on her throat, trickling down her neck, plastering her hair to her cheeks. Rain splashing on long puddles that jerked ahead of her, running parallel like two tracks, broken occasionally by patches of mud, in which her shoes squelched and slid, spattering her legs and skirt, wrenching her ankles; but she couldn't stop, couldn't slow down even, not until distance had swallowed up the building behind her and with it all hope of return.

Sweat ran down her forehead. Her breath came in gasps, each one tightening her chest with pain. Darkness paled as her eyes adapted, revealing twisted, blackened stumps lining the road and between them, scatterings of debris: old boxes, rusting barbed wire, bits of cloth and netting, even broken up two-wheeled carriages. And beyond these…

Nothing. A vast expanse of mud broken only by enormous craters brimming over with rain. Not a blade of grass, not a tree, not even a patch of stone to catch the eye. Slowing, she turned round. No sign of the bright, fire-lit room she'd left, the warmth, the dryness, the friends…

No. Don't think about that. Don't think. This is it now. Where you belong.

Belong. How could anyone belong in such emptiness? Where there was nowhere to be and no sound save for the water splashing on puddles and a distant rumble of thunder she'd barely noticed before but which now grew louder all the time…

Not thunder. Her stomach lurched. In the same moment a flash lit up the darkness, outlining the jagged shapes of tree stumps and twisted iron stakes in a strange orange glow, like a flare.

A *flare*. What soldiers sent up to show targets for the guns. She could be within range! Out of here, quick, retrace steps – another flash, followed by an ear-splitting crack. With a scream she hit the ground, spluttering as mud and water spurted into her mouth. More guns, from behind this time, sending a sound like a huge train screeching through the air above to explode in a shower of red in the distance.

The guns were behind her. No going back, then. What should she do, where could she go? In the slowly fading light her eyes darted from shape to shape. Somewhere, something must give shelter, even if only a dip in the ground or a curve of the landscape… *there*. Less than twenty metres away, to the left of the road, a dark, uneven mass snaking away, mounds created not by explosions but by deliberate spadework, glimpses of blackness in between. A trench! It couldn't be anything else.

With a squelch she pushed up to a crouching position and launched herself across the churned-up ground. Over the edge, sweatshirt and skirt twisting as she slid to the bottom – ah! Her feet hit cold water. For a moment she stayed, panting, arms outstretched against piled up sandbags, feeling the pressure of their solid shapes against her chest and their roughness on her cheek. Then, wiping her hand on a part of her sweatshirt not caked in mud, she pulled back the hair from her eyes and turned round.

The trench looked well made. That was something. Wooden struts supported the sides and duckboards partially covered puddles along the bottom. Sandbags, piled on each other like long flat khaki sausages, built up the opposite side higher than this one. That was good. More protection from the guns.

But not from the rain! She curled her toes, feeling the socks cling to her feet inside her shoes like soggy cardboard. She must keep moving. Find a dugout, a makeshift roof of corrugated iron, maybe, an area hollowed out from the side, *anything…*

Setting off, she splashed a few paces before turning a sharp corner. And another. Every few steps came another change of direction, with wires and sections of netting poking out of the ground to trip her up. Boxes lined the walls, mostly old ammunition ones; but some had red crosses painted on the sides. Her stomach jerked as a huge rat dragged its scaly tail along a pile of canvas and poles before disappearing into a patch of darkness on the right.

Clenching her teeth, she pressed on, treading more carefully. Drawing parallel with the dark area of wall, she breathed more easily; no sign of the rat. Instead, a turning led off at an angle, broken up by more twists and turns: a communication trench, probably, leading to – her heart froze. *To the front line.* A fire trench with a parapet and a step cut into the side, machine gun emplacements, snipers' posts… she shivered and turned away.

And yet – something didn't fit. A channel into the battle zone should be getting deeper, not shallower; but from the few visible metres of this one, the walls were losing height. Not far beyond, patches of water shimmered at ground level.

A picture flashed across her mind with a force that knocked her off balance. She gripped the side of the trench to steady herself, mud oozing through her fingers.

This was Passchendaele. No intricate network of tunnels and shelters, whole dwelling stations built under-ground, like in some stretches of the western front. Not in the wetlands of Flanders. Here the front line didn't exist. Just a sea of mud and water where only shell holes gave protection and if you lost your footing you drowned.

A wave of nausea rose inside her and she closed her eyes. Seconds later, she wrenched them open as a blaze of light lit up her surroundings in sharp relief. A crack of guns, louder than before; she threw herself into the mud as missiles hissed above her head, exploding beyond the trench, how close she couldn't tell but it felt close enough. Oh, if only she could get under cover, *real* cover! This trench at least had been dug deep enough, for god's sake! Surely somewhere…

A shape caught her eye. In the flare's lingering glow a black rectangle, framed by wooden struts, stood out on the left a few paces away. A dugout, it must be! Her breath came in a rush as she stumbled towards it, feeling for the rough edge of the timber support as it turned inwards – *yes*. Darkness that smelt of damp earth and clay. Beams supporting a low ceiling, a sharp turn after a couple of metres into – into what? Stretching her eyes wide, she stared into the gloom.

It was no good. Without the bough – *no. Don't think about that.* She shook herself. Without a *torch* – that was more like it – she could go no further.

Well. If that's the way it was, she'd have to get used to it. At least – she glanced back to the opening – some light entered that way. And here at last was a resting place, a dugout to shelter in from rain as well as guns. If she could just find something to sit on…

Yes, and what then? Sit down and wait for – what? For it all to be over? Because this wasn't just a bit of bad weather to sit out, a spot of bother between neighbours, this was *it* now. Forever. *Forever.* What part of that word didn't she understand?

She clenched her fists so tight the nails cut into her skin. Good. Let them. Give her something else to think about. Otherwise she'd go crazy. Relaxing her fingers, she took a few deep breaths. That was better. She must just take one thing at a time.

In the dim light of the inner passage she could just make out a large box. That would do for a seat. As she tugged it towards the entrance, her hand brushed a cold, hard shape lying on the top and she let out a gasp. That curve of metal tubing, opening out to a bell, it *couldn't* be…

She lifted it. Light filtering in from distant flares caught the gleam of brass. A trumpet all right, but a strange one: just a long piece of tubing curled round on itself, a mouthpiece at one end, the bell at the other, no valves – of course! It was a bugle. Her mouth twitched into a smile as she settled on the box. Here was a challenge. She raised the instrument to her lips.

It was hard at first to get the pressure right. But after a few stifled blasts her lip muscles adjusted and two notes rose pure and clear, just as they had only, what – hours ago? Days? She couldn't tell. In a different world, on the bank of a river with trees waving, green grass and brown earth, bright blue jumpers over grey uniforms, splashes of scarlet poppies, a kaleidoscope of colour… She breathed and blew again, the same notes and one a third higher, followed by the brief, mournful cascade –

From far away a single, desolate cry rang out.

'Kill!'

CHAPTER TWENTY-FIVE

In the Dugout

The bugle fell to her lap. She sat hunched, not daring to move, pressing her fingers against the metal so hard the blood fled from the tips.

'Kill! *Ki-i-ill!*'

It came from the battlefield.

Ante's heart beat against her ribs. She didn't breathe. Someone was out there! Leaning forwards, she strained to hear the cry come again or – what would be worse – answering yells and shouts, coming from other soldiers, a whole army trained to kill. Oh god, had they heard her? Had she found a place of shelter only to give herself away?

The bugle shook in her hands. Slipping off the box, she laid it down and peered outside. Instantly she shrank back. Noises – and much closer! A splashing and squelching, a grunt as someone tripped over… more soldiers, coming down the trench, *coming to get her!* Would they be ghosts? Spectres? Gripping the wooden struts of the dugout wall, she fought down the scream rising inside her.

Other sounds mingled with the shuffling. The most beautiful sounds in the world.

' – and I said I don't believe you. She's a *girl*.'

'Oh, so only boys can play the trumpet, is that it?'

Ante stumbled out of the dugout, sobs bursting in her throat. Two grey-streaked figures jumped back: one sturdy, pale-faced, his lank hair plastered flat to his head, the other slight, fine-featured, large blue eyes blinking out of sockets caked in mud.

'*Ante!*' Florence raised her arm and a glow suffused the gloom around her. 'It led us to you, I knew it would!'

Warmth blazed on her skin as Ante fell forward, past the bough, burying her face in a soft shoulder that smelt of damp cotton and earth. Behind her came something between a cry and a groan, then Gil's weight against her side, his arms round both of them and for a moment she held on tightly, not caring about the filth and the cold splashing of the rain.

'It – it's good to see you,' Florence gasped in her ear, 'but I've got to breathe.'

Ante released her at once. 'Sorry,' she mumbled. 'I – I just can't believe it. You came out here – both of you' – her eyes shot to Gil who grinned back, catching his breath – 'when you could be somewhere much nicer. You don't belong here. Not – not like *me* – ' tears blocked her throat.

'No, but that was all crap!' Grasping her shoulders, Florence tilted her face upwards, forcing their eyes to meet. 'You don't belong here either! That complete psycho – the Devil – said so after you'd gone.'

'What?' A wild hope seized Ante. She didn't dare believe it. 'What did he say?'

'It was a trick. He wanted to see which one of us would crumble first. He'd have put money on it being you, he said, because of your mistaken conviction that you'd murdered me. Saw it the moment you entered the room.'

'*Mistaken*?' Something bubbled up inside Ante.

Florence nodded. 'So we asked him which of us it was meant to be and he just shrugged. Since you'd offered yourself, why should we care? We were free. That's when we came after you.'

The words whirled in Ante's brain. She barely heard them. They were nothing to the one simple certainty that made her want to shout and laugh and cry all at once. 'Then you're alive! You didn't fall!'

Florence opened her mouth to reply and stopped, a strange expression on her face.

The wave in Ante's veins ebbed. 'Isn't that what he said?'

'Of course.' Florence nodded, briefly closing her eyes. 'Well, not exactly. But I'm sure that's what he meant. So,' she hurried on, 'nice place you've got here. You going to ask us in or what?'

Ante felt her face crack into a smile. Never mind the questions still unanswered, they were all together again, that was what mattered. Anything was possible.

Lightness filled her chest as she led them into the dugout, the bough's gleam now revealing a small underground room, only just high enough to stand up in. Against one wall stood a table with two rickety chairs and several wooden boxes around it, some open, some turned upside down to provide seats. Metal glinted from one of the open boxes and Florence bent to look.

'Ration cans,' she said. 'That's – weird. When there's no one here. And look: loads of other stuff.' The beam of light travelled round the edges of the room, falling on shelves bearing enamel plates and cups, tins, even four dusty wine glasses.

No one here. Ante stood still. That cry – she'd completely forgotten it. Tensing, she listened into the darkness. After a moment her shoulders relaxed. Whatever it was, it had stopped. Perhaps she'd even conjured it up herself, the thought of being utterly alone forever doing strange things to her mind... well, that wouldn't happen now.

'This must be the officers' quarters,' said Gil, moving a pile of greatcoats from where they lay draped over a box, so he could sit on it. 'Better than out there at any rate. Though if anyone'd told me this is what the next war would be like I'd never have believed him.' He uncorked his waterskin and fumbled at its coating of mud before giving up and lifting it to his lips.

Water. Ante's tongue felt dry. Taking one of the chairs she drank from her own supply, forcing herself to stop after only a couple of gulps. The skin felt alarmingly light. Soon they'd run out and then what? A picture leapt into her mind of craters brimful and overflowing with dark, foaming liquid. Her stomach churned.

'What's through there?' Pressing the cork back in, Gil nodded to a dark doorway at the far side of the room.

Florence broke off her exploration of the shelves to stretch her arm through the opening. 'Bunk beds.' Plonking herself into the chair opposite Ante, she drank from her waterskin. 'Only two, though. We'll have to share.'

'Or take turns,' said Ante. 'Mustn't fight over it.'

Florence's eyes shot to hers and creased up.

Ante smiled back. It wasn't that funny but who cared. Whatever it took to get them through the days, the nights – if day and night even existed here and it wasn't just one long, long twilight stretching on forever…

'Speaking of turns,' said Florence, 'here.' She held out the bough. 'You should have this, now we're together again.'

Ante waved her hand. 'It's OK,' she murmured. 'Later maybe.'

Her head and shoulders sank against the wall. For a moment she felt the hardness of the timbers against her scalp; then nothing.

★ ★ ★

She snapped awake. Stillness around her. Before her on

the table Florence lay slumped, a gleam from the bough catching her hair, fingers curled either side of her head, motionless save for the slight rise and fall of breathing. Whatever had woken Ante, it hadn't come from Florence.

Yet something had woken her. Something urgent, desperate, piercing the depths of her sleep and wrenching her mind to the surface. A sound she'd heard before, not long ago.

Oh god. That was it.

She sat up, blinking, her limbs stiff with cold, and listened into the darkness. Couldn't the others hear him? Wait a minute, how could *she* hear him? That a single cry would travel all the way from no man's land, down the trenches to reach them here, deep in the earth! Maybe she really was going crazy. If it came again, and neither Florence nor Gil stirred –

Her heart stopped. The box where Gil had sat lay empty.

No time to think. Seizing the bough from the table, she stumbled out of the dugout and down the passage. At the opening she gasped; the rain had stopped but an icy wind gusted down the trench, rippling the puddles. Screwing her eyes up, she stared into the gloom. *There he was.* A dozen paces away, at the junction between the two trenches.

'Gil!'

He turned. In the light of the bough the grey eyes stared through her before sliding away.

Coldness gripped her. Something was wrong. 'Where are you going?'

'To him.' Gil's head jerked. He clenched his hands to his sides as if only that way could he hold himself back long enough to reply. 'Can't you hear? Got to help him.' He disappeared through the opening.

Ante shot after him and seized his sleeve. 'What are you talking about? Help who?' she yelled. 'You can't go out there, you'll be blown to pieces!'

He pulled away from her. 'No I won't. Haven't you noticed? It's stopped.'

He was right. The hiss and shriek of shells, the whine of shrapnel, the tremendous thud of explosions in the distance – all had ceased with the rain. In the silence rats scuffled among storage boxes, with the occasional plop as one fell into the water.

'Must be a truce,' Gil muttered. 'Between who I don't know. I haven't the faintest idea what the war is about or who we're fighting – though Florence did try to explain it to me – and I don't care. All I know is that he's out there, wounded, and I've got to help him.' He set off down the trench.

'Who? Gil, wait!' She must stop him at all costs. 'You don't know how long the truce – if there is one – will last. This is the Devil's idea of fun, remember. He'll probably start it all up again the minute you – '

'There!' At the first turn he shot round, wincing as the same anguished cry broke through the air. 'He's calling me! You can hear him, I know you can! Not

Florence; she's not – not ready yet. But *you* – ' he broke off, his eyes searching her face. 'You understand. You have to.'

She stared back at him. Had he gone mad? '*Me*? What do I understand?'

The muscles of his jaw worked for a second. 'Doesn't matter.' Shaking his head, he vanished round the corner.

This was lunacy! She should run, make him come back, or grab Florence and get her to help. But her legs wouldn't move. She stayed fixed to the spot, Gil's words circling and tumbling through her brain.

A tug on her arm. 'What's going on? Was that Gil? What the hell's he doing?'

'Florence!' The blood seemed to course through her once more. 'He's gone out there, alone, with *nothing*, with some crazy idea of rescuing someone – he's totally lost it!'

The grip on her sleeve tightened. Florence stood, shoulders hunched, eyes on the blank mud wall a few metres away. 'So what do we do?' she whispered.

★ ★ ★

Ten minutes. It couldn't have taken more than that. Time to struggle into one of the greatcoats – heavy, scratchy, down to her ankles, but warm – and unhook a steel helmet from the wall.

'Here, take this.' Florence handed her a bulky shape on a long strap.

Ante raised her eyebrows. 'What is it?'

'Gas masks.' Florence hung two around her neck, trying not to tangle them in the thick collar of her coat. 'I found them before. We may need them.'

Ante seized the box. *Poison gas.* And Gil was out there with no mask, no helmet, nothing but his battered school uniform to protect him... Attaching a spare helmet to her gas mask strap, she made for the way out.

'I still don't understand,' Florence panted behind her. 'If there really is some poor guy out there calling for help – *if* – why didn't Gil wait to tell us? We could've worked out what to do together.'

'It wasn't even a call for help,' said Ante. 'It was a call for – ' she stopped. *Kill...kill.* What an idiot she had been! Not *kill*...

Just a long, desolate plea for one person alone.

Gil. Gil. Gi-i-il.

CHAPTER TWENTY-SIX

Shapes in the Darkness

The wind bit into Ante's neck, bearing gusts of sleet that froze her skin. After the first twist the trench grew rapidly shallower, giving less protection from the weather. She turned up the collar of her greatcoat, wrapping the cloth tightly round her body, trying not to think about her feet, soaked through already and numb with cold. Nor about Gil, out there somewhere, bareheaded, legs pale under his flannel jacket and shorts…

One metre, half a metre, now – no difference at all. A duckboard track snaked away across a vast, colourless – what? Ante stared into the gloom, straining her eyes till she had to blink, while her stomach seemed to shrink inside her. You couldn't call it a landscape. A sea of mud broken into solid, chopped up waves stood out against the darkness, interspersed with great water-filled craters, all overlapping each other so that not a single piece of ground anywhere remained that hadn't been churned up and spewed out into a new, alien shape. Not even tree stumps remained here. But in the light of the flares other shapes stood out: broken carts, clumps of barbed wire, rusting sheets of corrugated iron, machine gun belts, rifles, and everywhere, thousands and thousands of shell cases and pieces of metal.

And there was worse.

As she led the way down the track, she saw them. Dead bodies. Piles of dead bodies. Lying face down in slimy water, swollen beyond all recognition, their limbs bent back crazily. And rising out of the craters a terrible, stomach-churning smell…

'I'm going to be sick.' Florence bent double, one hand clasped to her mouth. 'We – can't – go – on – in – this.'

'We have to.' Ante heard her voice sound weirdly high. She swallowed. 'Keep looking ahead.'

One step, two – a gap in the duckboards – concentrate on *that*, Ante told herself, not on the shapes that lay on either side of the track, crowding into her mind. She bit her lips together. *Focus on what's in front of you. Don't think about them. They're dead. Nothing you can do for them.*

A flash lit up the darkness. She threw herself to the ground. Shells screamed and exploded to her left, sending up fountains of mud, bits of wood and metal. Something pinged on her helmet, followed by flop! flop! as pieces of shrapnel and shell-casing came raining down, splashing in the mud. Icy water soaked into her clothes as she lay on the track, not daring to move, clamping her teeth to stop herself from screaming and choking on mud and filth.

'*Ante!*' Florence's voice came close to her ear. 'What do we do? What the hell do we do?'

'He's started it again, I knew he would,' she yelled back. 'Lie low!'

They huddled together, shaking with cold and fear until the rage died down. A cold breeze blew up, bringing the sharp, dry smell of explosives to their nostrils, followed by large drops of water as it began to rain.

Florence shivered and clutched Ante even more tightly than before. 'So wh-what do you reckon? D-do we stay here and f-f-freeze until we drown, or do we g-get up and get bl-blown to bits – '

'Ssh.'

Straight ahead down the track, a figure moved through the smoke towards them. It walked unsteadily, slipping in the mud, breathing hard with every step.

Florence gave a little shriek, tried to scramble to her feet and slipped back into the mud with a horrible sucking sound. Ante rolled over on to her side to extract the bough from underneath her and held it up to reveal a face, white with shock, and two startled grey eyes under a mop of sandy hair.

'Gil!' cried Florence. 'Thank God! Where have you *been* – '

Her voice trailed away. Gil stood swaying, mouth open as if to speak, but no sound came. His face was caked in mud, through which his eyes stared unblinkingly. One sleeve of his jacket hung torn at the shoulder and blood trickled down to his lower arm. Hideous pink, raw blisters covered his skin from elbow to wrist.

Ante cried out. 'Gil, you're hurt! Come back with us, we'll find some – some bandages, or – ' she stopped. His wounds needed much more than that. What could they do?

He sank to his knees on the duckboard. 'Bandages,' he murmured. 'No. A stretcher.'

'A stretcher?' cried Florence. 'But Gil, it's your arm that's – '

'Not for me.' He waved his hand, wincing with pain. 'For him. I've found him. In a shell-hole back there.'

'Who?' said Ante.

Gil raised his eyes to her face. 'You know who. It's – well, it's – you.'

'*Me*?' Ante gaped. Beside her Florence breathed in sharply and shrank back.

Shell shock, it must be. He was hallucinating. Slowly, so as not to frighten him, Ante reached out her hand to touch him. 'I'm OK, Gil. Look. I'm here.'

'No.' He seemed to come to himself. 'I – I didn't mean that. It's my – ' he broke off and struggled to his feet. 'He's wounded. Got to get a stretcher.' He stumbled past her down the track.

Ante gasped. The look in Gil's eyes, the mumbled explanation that made no sense… Somewhere in her memory an echo sounded, melting away as she tried to grasp it. Never mind, no time for that now. 'Gil, wait!'

They mustn't lose him. Not in this state. If it meant playing along, she'd do it. 'If you really have found this guy' – she looked at Florence, who nodded – 'let us go for the stretcher. You come back to the dugout and we'll try and find something for your arm.'

He swivelled round. 'Will you really?' He straightened up, as if her words had given him a burst of strength. 'Then I'll wait with him. Forget my arm' – he rushed on, as she opened her mouth to protest – 'it's only a bit of shrapnel. But then I fell into a shell hole and there was some sort of green slime covering the water.'

Poison gas. Anger surged through Ante and her eyes flew to Florence's. The Devil hadn't missed a single detail.

'Gil, wait.' With a squelching sound Florence pulled herself out of the mud. 'Take this.' She handed him the spare satchel from round her neck. 'It's a gas mask. You may need it.'

'A *gas* mask?'

'And this,' said Ante, scrambling to her feet and holding out the helmet.

He took the offerings with a dazed air; the helmet, at least, he knew what to do with. Strapping it on, he called back over his shoulder, 'Please hurry! I must go back to him.'

Then he was off in the direction he'd come, stumbling and slipping down the track.

'A stretcher,' sighed Florence. 'Where'll we find that?'

'Not in the dugout,' said Ante. 'We'd have seen it.

Somewhere long enough for – '

She stopped. An image rose before her, a wall of mud held back with netting, red cross boxes leaning against it and two metal poles lying on top, canvas folded between them.

'I know,' she said.

CHAPTER TWENTY-SEVEN

'I died in Hell –
(They called it Passchendaele)'

Siegfried Sassoon

The crater was vast. A dark, jagged wound gouged out of the sodden ground, it sloped upwards to meet them as Ante, her lungs drawing deep gasps of air, flung herself into it, hands gripping the stretcher poles. A cry from behind and she felt the poles drop as Florence briefly lost her hold; then the weight steadied again. Pole ends pressing into her chest, she lay panting full length in the mud, Florence's breath coming in short gasps behind her.

'You made it!' Lying on his elbows a short distance away, Gil waved the rifle he held propped in front of him. The steel helmet balanced on the barrel clanged gently. Close up, Ante shuddered. He'd had to find some way of guiding them but the risk was huge: bullet marks scored the helmet all over. Her eye moved to the rest of him. The burn on his arm looked uglier than ever and blood now streaked his face as well as his shoulder. She swallowed hard.

But in his delight at seeing them, Gil seemed to feel no pain. 'Follow me!' Strapping his helmet back on he half slid, half crawled past them down the crater.

'Gil!' Florence had only just got her breath back. 'Oh, what's the use.'

Crouching sideways on the slope so as not to fall, Ante steered the poles to follow Gil, bobbing just below her, towards a dark mass filling the bottom of the crater. As they got closer, her stomach lurched. Water had collected into a deep pool, heavy with mud and, in places, with blood as well. Around the edge of the pool lay half-submerged shapes of terrible suffering: limbs twisted and mangled, faces bloated and rotten or with white teeth bared, the flesh completely burnt away. The smell of decay, sweet and sickening, hung on the air.

Nausea welled up inside her. Out of the corner of her eye she saw Florence turn aside, drop the stretcher poles, and choke uncontrollably, her shoulders shaking. Gulping down the saliva filling her own mouth she was about to call on Gil to stop – when she realised he *had* stopped and was looking back up at them.

And lying next to him was a young, slightly-built soldier with a tangle of blood and flesh where his leg should be. Light from the bough fell on a deathly-pale face and brown eyes clouded with pain.

Ante screamed. The stretcher fell to the ground as she clasped her face in her hands. 'This is him? Lying here, calling for help – for *you* – ' her eyes sought Gil's but he looked away. 'Then – *how many more are there?*' Her gaze darted to the twisted, mud-streaked shapes breaking the surface of the water below. 'Still alive, still in pain, forever and *ever* – ' she stopped, strangled by sobs.

Then the warmth of Gil's arm round her shoulders and his voice in her ear. 'No more. They're all dead, the others. They aren't even real. Look, those down there – '

'No, no I can't look again!'

'Well I have. I had to check. But when I' – he paused – 'when I touched them I – I nearly jumped out of my skin. There was nothing there. They're just shadows.'

'Oh.' She let out a long, shaky breath.

'Then he called me again. And this time I found him.'

'But – but who is he?' Florence, pale and with dark circles around her eyes, glanced at the wounded soldier. 'And why's he real and not the others?'

A long, low moan erupted from the young man. His lips, parched and colourless, moved as if he were trying to speak.

Gil's eyes shot from him to Florence and Ante and back again. 'Look, I can't explain now. We've got to get him away. He's been lying here in that – in that state for a long time. A very long time.'

'Gil!' protested Ante, 'we're not doctors. What can we do to help him? Where can we take him? Gil, please, *listen* – '

But he'd already picked up one end of the stretcher and was dragging it alongside the wounded man. 'If we hold it down the slope, just below him, like this, we can slide him into it.'

'Yes, but Gil,' said Florence, 'have you any idea how awkward this thing is when it's empty? How'll we manage when it's full and we have to get back through all that mud and shelling?'

He sat back on his heels. 'I – I don't know, we've just *got* to. There'll be three of us, remember. And at least he's not very big. *Please.*'

A spasm of pain shot through his face as he bent down and grasped the soldier underneath the shoulders. Florence, averting her gaze from the blood-soaked leg, tentatively stretched out her hands, her fingers tiny against his body.

This is madness, thought Ante. But one glance into Gil's eyes and she knelt down, grasping the wounded man near his mangled leg with all the strength and lightness she could muster. Together they somehow moved him on to the stretcher, fastening the stiff, leather straps across his body, shrinking back at his moans of pain.

'We're just hurting him more!' cried Florence.

The dry, cracked lips pressed together.

'He needs water,' said Ante. Uncorking her supply, she slid her arm under the young man's head and held it to his lips. His face relaxed and for a moment she forgot the ache in her shoulders. Straightening up again, she sealed the waterskin, trying not to notice how limp it now hung, nor the thirst creeping into her own throat.

Pain shot through her arms as she took up her side of the stretcher. Beside her Florence struggled with the other pole while at the head Gil fought to keep his balance, as he led them, slipping and sliding, up the slope to ease themselves and their burden over the lip of the crater. A moment to catch their breath; then they started down the duckboard track.

Mud pulled at each footstep. Rain spattered off Ante's helmet and trickled in cold streams down her neck. Before her the lower part of the soldier's face, unprotected by his helmet, gleamed gaunt and hollow. If only they could get him under cover, away from weather and guns alike! She glanced ahead. The trench wasn't that far away. Near enough, if the shelling didn't turn in their direction again. She sank her head into the collar of her coat, ears straining for the first sign of change in the distant boom of the guns. Ahead, the tendons in Gil's wrists stood out above his hands gripping the poles.

Wisps of smoke drifted over the wasteland, blotting out whole sections of duckboard. She fixed her eyes on Gil's back as he staggered to follow the twists and turns in the track. That would be worse than anything! To lose their way or their footing; to be swallowed up and drowned in mud like the dim, half-sunk shapes around them – she clenched her fingers around her end of the pole. *Breathe calmly. Don't think about it.* Her back hurt enough already; tensing up would make it worse.

There, at last, only a short distance away: the dip in the ground that meant the beginning of the trench. Her heart leapt. They were nearly home and dry.

A crack in the distance and a gentle plop on the ground a little way behind her. Not worth bothering about. Funny, though, this new smell rising above the shell fumes and stench of decomposing bodies: slightly acidic, chemical, mixed with a sweet flavour of pear. Almost pleasant, really.

A sharp pull at her shoulder as the pole beside her dropped to the ground. 'Hey, what – '

Florence tore at the box round her neck. 'It's gas, Ante, GAS, don't you realise? Gil, put your mask on!'

Gil let go of the stretcher and obeyed. Ante pulled off her helmet and thrust her mask over her head, fingers trembling as she fought to fix it in place. Breathing in, she nearly choked on air that came with difficulty, tasting of rubber and disinfectant. She turned to watch as Florence, looking like a giant mutant fly, with long proboscis curling down to the canvas bag on her chest, knelt over the soldier, fumbling to put his mask on for him.

Grasping the stretcher again, she lurched the last few steps into the trench. Through thick, green glass she glimpsed the bough throwing shadows on the walls, which grew taller as the trench deepened. Her neck ached with the weight of the canvas while her lungs felt they were going to burst, battling for air that became harder and harder to breathe. No, this was unbearable! If she didn't take it off right now, she was going to suffocate.

Her blood froze. A new, tingling sensation crept across her ears and round her neck, over skin not covered by canvas, while her hands, numb with cold, began to sting. Oh god, was that the gas? A choice then: suffocate or burn! Catching sight of Gil's bare, blistered right arm jerking ahead of her as he tried to hold the poles steady, her stomach tightened.

Reaching the junction with the support trench, Gil headed for the dugout. Ante looked at the opening. No good. They'd never get the stretcher in there. After a moment's hesitation, Gil ploughed on, steering them round the next turning before letting his end of the poles sink to the ground. With a nod to each other, they laid down the stretcher and tore off their gas masks.

Ante sniffed the air. It smelt sharp and cold; no trace of that strange chemical odour. Her shoulders relaxed. Letting out a long sigh, she watched as Florence bent to take off the soldier's mask. Two glittering eyes stared back above swollen, cracked lips. Rain drops coursed down the hollow cheeks, dripping over a chin so fine as to be barely formed.

Ante caught her breath. He was young, hardly old enough to shave. A memory flashed across her vision; a battered, mud-streaked figure swaying in the gloom, a halting, stammered answer that made no sense. *You know who it is. It's you.*

Crazy. Gil was babbling, confused, didn't know what he was saying. Yet the words hung in her mind, mingling with other things he'd begun to say and never finished, just as the pale face before her set up echoes that faded before she could grasp what they meant. Somewhere in all this lay an answer, if only she could piece it together.

The soldier shivered. A pang shot through her and she seized her side of the stretcher. Whoever he was, they couldn't stop to find out now. He needed shelter. If they carried on they might find another dugout, a wider one, or even a cavity scooped out of the wall: anywhere to lay him down out of the rain. There'd be time enough for riddle-solving then.

Beside her Florence pushed the tangled hair back from her eyes and picked up her pole. Glancing at her pale, drawn face, Ante tried to take the greater weight of their end of the stretcher, ignoring the pains shooting through her shoulder and neck at every turn. In each new section of trench, she scanned the sides for a possible opening to a dugout. But the walls continued on their uneven way, or descended into bombed-out troughs of crumbled mud, metal and splinters, before rising again, blank as before.

Gil stopped suddenly. 'Listen.'

Ante's heart pounded in her ears. She stood, feeling her chest rise and fall, waiting for her breathing to die down so she could hear – what? Nothing. Nothing! No guns. Or at most, a distant rumbling in the ground.

Something lifted inside her, releasing her tense, aching shoulders and sending a current through her veins. They'd left the battle behind.

Not only that. The trench was straighter than before, the frequent twists and turns petering out. Walking grew easier as their path widened and – she hardly dared believe it – began to slope uphill, leading them away from the waterlogged ground. And there, at last, just as the rain began to fall more gently, a sheet of corrugated iron spanned the trench high above their heads. Beneath it, metal boxes laid end to end lined both walls.

Not much of a shelter. But it would do.

Laying the two poles down on one length of the boxes, Gil flung himself down opposite, panting. Florence sank on to the makeshift seat at the foot of the stretcher while Ante moved round to the head. Leaning back against the wall, she closed her eyes. 'All right, Gil,' she sighed. 'Explain. Who is this poor guy?'

CHAPTER TWENTY-EIGHT

Harry

'He's my brother,' said Gil.

Ante and Florence stared at him. 'Your brother?' exclaimed Ante, 'But how – '

She was interrupted by a faint voice.

'Rifleman – Harry – Marow. First battalion – Rifle Brigade.' Feebly, the soldier tried to raise himself into a sitting position, gave up and sank back, exhausted.

Florence looked from the soldier to Gil. 'Your *brother*! Why on earth would your brother be in Hell?'

Staring at the ground, Gil blinked hard and didn't reply. His mouth moved, as if he were trying to frame words that refused to come.

'And calling for you,' said Ante.

'Because' – Gil's voice came so low it was barely audible – 'because maybe he hoped one day I'd come for him. Put things right. And when the – the Devil told me he was out there, I knew that of all of us, I was the one to go through his stupid door. Not – not you, Ante. I shouldn't have let you.'

Ante felt something tug at her chest as the grey eyes

looked up at last and met hers. She didn't breathe.

'What?' Florence's gaze darted from Ante to Gil. 'The Devil never mentioned your brother.'

'He said that Harry was out there,' murmured Ante. 'Killed at Passchendaele.'

Fragments at the back of her mind began to move. Sentences begun and never finished, snatches of words broken off or changed to others that made no sense…

'But – but Harry was the bully who murdered you,' whispered Florence. 'You said so yourself.'

Ante's heart beat faster. Pieces of the jigsaw fell into place. A stocky, sandy-haired school boy sitting hunched on a hillside beside her, tugging at tufts of grass, flinging them savagely away. *Pushed over the hand rail. By – another boy.*

Not just any other boy. *By my brother.*

Florence's eyes searched Gil's face. 'Are you saying' – she snatched a glance at the slight figure lying beside her, whose own gaze flickered but remained fixed on Gil – '*your own brother murdered you?*'

Gil blinked at his mud-streaked hands. 'It wasn't murder. I drove him to it.'

Silence. Ante gripped the edge of her seat and looked down at the ground. Out of the corner of her eye she saw the soldier's face tighten, as if with a spasm of pain.

'OK Gil,' said Florence. 'You'd better tell us what really happened.'

Gil shifted on his seat, opening and shutting his mouth several times. 'It was the tradition for new boys,' he began at last. 'They had to pass a test before we'd accept them, show they weren't cowards or cry babies. And Harry – well, he was a milksop, he'd been crying every night since term began. It was embarrassing. I mean' – he drew himself up – 'I'd started Northwell's at his age three years before and *I'd* never made such a fuss.'

'So he was younger than you,' broke in Ante. 'He's your *little* brother. Not a big, mean guy.'

Her gaze flew back to the stretcher. The glittering eyes were tight shut, the mouth a thin, taut line, as if trying to keep back more than physical pain.

Gil reddened and slumped back into his former hunched position. 'Yes. He – he was actually quite a lot smaller than me, small even for a ten year-old.' He cringed at this thought, his voice failing briefly.

'Go on,' prompted Florence.

'He was letting me down. It was my job to think up what his initiation test should be. I knew I had to make it really tough, otherwise the other boys would say I'd been soft on him. So I – so I hit on the organ loft. I and a couple of the other fellows made him get up in the middle of the night and come with us.'

'And then – ?' Ante leaned forward.

'I told him to get over the hand rail at one end and climb along the outside to the other. He kicked up a terrible fuss, said he was scared of heights, started snivelling and crying all over the place. I should have stopped then, I know, I could see it was all going wrong

210

but I *couldn't* back off with the other fellows there laughing and jeering. So I – I – '

' – forced him.' Ante couldn't meet Gil's eye. Her cheek burnt under Gil's gaze, willing her to look back, but she did not.

Gil licked his lips. His voice sank to a whisper. 'Yes. I picked him up – he was quite light, you see – and I – I held him over the edge. I was leaning right over, trying to get him to grip on to the railings and he was clinging to me, when suddenly he stopped resisting and grabbed the hand rail. Good, I thought, battle over. Then his left foot slipped and as I bent down to reposition it, he kicked out at me, hard. I lost my balance and went straight over, head first on to the stone floor.'

A long silence fell, broken only by the drumming of the rain on the corrugated iron over their heads. Ante gazed down at Harry's pale, gaunt face, marked with pain, and imagined the terrified little boy he had been.

'So that's how it was,' she said. 'You were bullying him. Not the other way round.'

Gil nodded, unable to look at her.

'How *could* you?' Words rushed through her, too fast to contain. 'Your own brother! No wonder he wanted to kill you – ' She stopped. Inside her chest the wave broke and fell away, leaving only emptiness.

Like she'd wanted something to happen to Florence. Was that what Gil had meant, out there in no man's land? *You know who it is. It's you.*

He was warning her. Because killing a friend was pretty close to killing your brother.

And she'd thought he was raving.

She began to tremble and dug her nails into the folds of her coat. Dimly she saw the figure opposite crumple up as if he'd been punched in the stomach, face buried in his hands.

She blinked. Secrets, half-truths, more fragments coming together. Something wobbled at the back of her throat but she couldn't hold back now. 'So, Gil,' she began, 'you worked it out. What this has all been about. You and Harry' – she nodded towards the wounded soldier – 'Florence and me. What I want to hear is – how long have you known? From back there, in the Devil's headquarters? Or' – she felt her voice harden – '*right from the start?* Of course, that's it! In the organ loft. When it looked as if I was going to do the same to Florence as Harry did to you, that's when you intervened!'

'Oh Gil,' said Florence. 'I wish you'd told us. Everything would've made more sense then.'

The figure lying beside Ante twitched. From the tilt of his head he longed to turn right round to look at her. His gaze focussed on Florence instead.

Gil snatched his hands from his face. His skin was smeared and blotchy, his pale lashes stuck together in dark tufts. Blinking, his eyes sought Ante's. 'It wasn't like that, I swear! I didn't *intervene*, it just happened. And it never occurred to me to see a connection between us. I just thought you two were having some kind of argument. You weren't beating each other up, not like me and Harry.' He paused, seeming to grapple with his thoughts. 'It wasn't till that moment in the tunnel, when – when I stopped Florence going over the precipice and she was fighting me off, tearing and scratching and kicking, that it flashed into my head that this was me and Harry and I thought – I thought, oh, if only it *was*' – his voice cracked – 'and I was *saving* Harry instead of making him do something he'd never, never have – ' he choked and stared blindly down at his hands, clenched into fists so tight the knuckles showed white under streaks of mud.

Ante felt a rawness in her throat. 'Gil – '

On the stretcher something moved. A hand, caked in mud and blood, reached out and touched Gil on the knee. For a split second Gil stared at Harry in disbelief; then he grasped the hand and bowed over it, his face hidden.

'Gil,' whispered Harry. 'Gil.'

When at last he straightened up, his hand still in his brother's, it seemed to Ante that Gil had aged several years. A strange feeling, somewhere between warmth and longing, swept through her. They'd found each other, made up for the past. Whatever happened now, they'd be together.

Glancing at Florence, she was surprised to find the blue gaze resting not on what was happening between Gil and Harry, but on her, with an expression she couldn't fathom. Yet she'd seen that look before, not long ago…yes. Outside the dugout, Florence drawing back from her embrace, assuring her she was still alive – while the opposite possibility lay in her eyes.

Ante's shoes, grey and caked with mud, melted to a blur. What did it matter, exactly what happened in the organ loft? If Florence was dead, she'd as good as killed her, whatever word you used. *Killed her.* Heat stung her eyes and she shut them tight.

A cry wrenched them open. Florence was staring at Gil in horror. 'Gil! Your legs, your *skin*! Oh it looks *horrible.*'

Gil looked down at himself. Great red blisters covered his bare legs; some had already burst, leaking burning yellow fluid on to other parts of his skin. A raw, red rash spread over his neck, shoulder and waist where his jacket hung loose and torn – in fact over all parts of his body exposed to the icy air. When he raised his face to them again, fear as well as pain filled his eyes.

'It was that gas shell,' said Florence, 'it burns the skin as well as the lungs. Ante and me were lucky: we've got coats on. Oh, Gil…' her voice trailed away as her gaze turned first to Harry, then to Ante. Two of them, now, it said. What do we do?

The sides of Gil's mouth cracked as he tried to lick his lips. His hand went for his kidskin and fell away, leaving it hanging limp and empty across his chest.

'Water.' Ante stood up, wincing as her frozen feet took the weight of her body. 'We have to find fresh water. I know,' she rushed on, seeing the doubt in their eyes, 'there's been none since Elysium. But the ground is starting to slope upwards. It hasn't done that before. If we follow it, even just for a bit, we may come to a stream. It's our only hope.'

★ ★ ★

Step after step, muscles screaming in protest in her shoulders, her arms, her back, fingers bent like claws, pain shooting through her feet, swollen and numb with cold – *let it.* Let the sheer physical agony flood her mind; that way there'd be no room for other thoughts. The ones that poured in no matter what she did.

You didn't murder Florence, her brain chanted. *So she is still alive.* But then the memory of Florence's face, back there by the dugout, her strange, unreadable expression, and the sudden vagueness of her words… *Well, not exactly. But I'm sure that's what he meant…*

No! She couldn't think about that now. The trench, concentrate on the trench. The going was getting tougher. The ground sloped upwards ever more steeply and the trench itself was petering out, becoming instead a muddy path, slippery and difficult to follow.

Gil and Harry. Florence and her. Mirror images of each other, a hundred years apart. What if the pattern went on? Their fight had released Gil from the organ loft: would Florence take his place? For the next hundred years, or until she was ready – ah! Was *that* what he meant, back there, on the edge of no man's land? *Not Florence; she's not ready yet. But you understand. You have to.* Because –

Her stomach turned to lead.

Because she, Ante, must return with the bough alone.

No, please, anything but that! Her eyes flew to the slight figure stumbling along beside her. A few tendrils of blonde hair still shone on Florence's forehead, the rest was caked in mud. Her cheek looked pale and drawn and her breath came rapidly as she struggled with her pole. Yet she seemed solid enough. But then so did Gil, on this side of the organ loft. It was on the other that he'd been a shadow.

Ante forced her gaze forwards again. *Stop thinking. Just stop it. It's all going to work out. It has to.* At least the path was getting easier, in spite of the uphill work. For a while now the great weight on each footstep had lightened as the soft mud dried up; now she trod on dry ground, still bare and grey, but *dry*. And it had stopped raining.

Little by little, the wind subsided. A new sound rose ahead, a different kind of rushing from the wind's, a sound that spoke of grass and leaves and smooth pebbles glinting in the sun. Ante let out a long sigh as a feeling almost of warmth spread through her limbs.

They were on it before she realised. The path curved round a small hillock and without warning, plunged downwards, becoming the steep bank of a fast-flowing river. Florence screamed as they slipped and slid

towards the foaming water. The muscles in Gil's wrists
and all the way up his bare, raw arm stood out as he
tried to force the stretcher back up the slope. Ante
pulled on her pole and, throwing all her weight behind
her, dug her heels hard into the ground.

No use. Streams of dry dust glided under their feet
and brought them crashing into the river. A wave shot
up and thundered on Gil's helmet, breaking over his
shoulders, braced at the last minute to take the blow.

'Lift him up, lift him up!' Gil fought to hold his end
of the stretcher, hunching in agony at the cold water
hitting his burning skin.

'I can't! I *can't*!' screamed Florence.

'We're losing him!' cried Ante.

She clenched her hands round the pole but the fast-
flowing stream forced itself between fingers and metal,
wrenching it from her grasp. Beside her Florence
staggered, arms flailing, as the weight of water pulled
the stretcher at last even from Gil. A glimpse of Harry's
eyes, wide open, darting; then the current spun him
round and sucked him down. Blood swirled on the
surface – and was gone.

'No – no – *NO!*' Ante's voice broke into a wail she
couldn't control.

They'd lost him. They'd struggled – twice – over that
landscape of mud and suffering, through shells
exploding and freezing cold, to rescue Harry – and for
what? To drown him, strapped helplessly to a stretcher
– how many ways could you die in Hell? Was this

another of the Devil's hideous jokes, his *supreme* joke, to make Gil think – to make them all think – they could put right what had gone wrong so many years ago?

She caught sight of Gil and the cry died in her throat. For Gil hadn't uttered a sound. He stood immobile before turning and looking at each of them, his eyes filled with something beyond sorrow, beyond despair even. Then, without a word, he waded deeper into the river.

'Gil!' cried Ante. 'Not you! Not you too!'

'Come back!' screamed Florence.

The water lapped at his shoulders, making his red and blistered skin gleam painfully bright. He didn't even stretch his arms out to swim as the current took him.

It was more than Ante could bear. She flung herself after him, gasping as the heavy folds of her greatcoat filled and dragged her down. Struggling, she wrenched her head round to stop Florence from following, but too late. She was just in time to see the last few tendrils of blonde hair disappearing under the water. Florence too was gone.

Ante tore her mouth open to cry out. A wall of water hit her throat, her windpipe, her lungs. She kicked frantically for the riverbed but her feet touched nothing.

CHAPTER TWENTY-NINE

The Far Shore

Grass. And warmth. The imprint of firm, dry ground the whole length of her body.

For several minutes she didn't move. Lying with her cheek on the soft grass, eyes shut tight so that the colour of sunlight inside the lids turned from orange to red, she breathed air laden with the scent of meadowsweet and clover.

Sunlight. The *sun*. Still not opening her eyes, Ante rolled on to her back and knew, with absolute certainty, that above her stretched no longer the dark, starless night of Hades, nor even the mysterious golden light of Elysium, but the clear sky of an early summer, cloudless and deep blue. Somewhere high above, a lark sang.

Then pain shot through her mind with the swiftness of a knife. Where she was meant nothing. Not when the best friends she'd ever known had just – had just – tears burnt her hot eyelids and she turned her face to the ground.

What comfort was it that she'd come through?

> *And bring you, when your journey's done*
> *To look again upon the sun.*

The bough had kept its promise all right. But at a cruel price.

A hand on her arm. Someone was shaking her roughly. 'Ante, look. Open your eyes, for goodness' sake.'

She sat up.

'At *last*.' Florence knelt on the grass between Ante and the river. Her hair was sleek and shining, her skin clean and unmarked.

Ante cried out. 'Florence, you're OK! *More* than OK. I can't believe – '

'It's the same for you too.'

She looked down at herself. It was true. Greatcoat, helmet, mask and kidskin had all disappeared. Her clothes, even her poor battered shoes, looked fresh and undamaged and her dark brown skin felt smooth and whole, all wounds and scratches gone. Gold flashed at her belt, so bright she screwed up her eyes.

'And Gil.'

Ante spun round.

A little way behind her, where the grass sloped upwards, stood Gil. In that ridiculous grey uniform, the sleeves of his jacket as good as new, all mud and blood washed away. He grinned at her, the freckles showing clearly once more on his pale skin, smooth and healthy with not a blister in sight.

She launched herself at his legs and nearly succeeded in bringing him down. 'Why didn't you *tell* me – '

'We tried – we called you,' he panted between guffaws. 'Didn't you hear?'

'No, I was too – '

'Hello.'

The voice was shy and tentative. Breaking off her tussle, Ante looked round to see a young man in khaki uniform standing at the edge of the river. Water poured off his clothes and darkened his thick hair, which when dry, she guessed, wouldn't be that different in colour from Gil's, perhaps a little redder. Taller than all of them, his slight build made him hardly more than a boy, yet the smile in his brown eyes betrayed a depth of pain beyond his years.

A little uncertainly, he stepped forward.

Gil, Ante and Florence erupted.

'*Harry!*'

'Your leg!'

'But you were dragged under!'

They fell on him, all trying to hug him at once, Ante and Florence showing Gil not the slightest respect for the fact that this was his brother, not theirs. Laughing, Harry allowed himself to be pulled up the riverbank to collapse in a heap with them all in the grass.

After a while Ante drew back, panting, and gazed from one face to another. It was too much to take in. Most of all – 'Your leg – I can't believe it,' she said, as her eyes kept flying back to Harry. 'It was completely smashed.'

He ran his hand down his left leg from knee to ankle and smiled.

'And you,' said Florence to Gil, 'those terrible burns.'

Gil grinned and shrugged. Ante felt the skin on her own shoulders prickle as she remembered the waves of pain this action would have sent through his body just a short time ago.

'I suppose,' said Harry, 'I suppose it must have something to do with the river. I thought it would be horrible to be pulled under water like that, trapped, unable to move, but – but it didn't feel like drowning. It felt – well, it felt as if I was letting go of everything and – and I was free.'

Ante nodded. A brief silence fell, broken only by the warm buzzing of bees and above them, the lark singing high in the sky.

Then Florence leapt to her feet and punched the air. 'We did it!' she cried. 'We rescued you!'

'You did,' agreed Harry. 'Thank you, Florence. And Ante,' he added, turning to her. 'Though how you two came to be involved in the first place – ' he stopped, his gaze flitting between them. 'Actually,' he continued, 'from listening to you back there' – he nodded across the river – 'I think I know why.'

Ante glanced at Florence and blushed. Florence met her gaze with a half-smile as crimson stole up her cheeks as well.

'So that's what it was, eh Gil?' said Harry. 'We two had to wait – you in the organ loft, me on the field of Passchendaele – for, let me see, how long? Months, years? Of course, it must have been a few years in your case, seven at lea – '

'A hundred,' said Gil.

Harry gaped. 'A – hundred?' Words seemed to dry in his mouth. 'I've been lying – in that shell hole – for *one hundred years*?'

'It didn't feel like it, then,' said Ante. 'Good.'

A hundred hours would be bad enough. Minutes, even.

Harry shook his head slowly. 'I know it sounds odd but – but I must have drifted into some kind of dream where everything around me just – stood still.'

'Not odd at all,' said Gil.

'The guns, the shells shrieking and exploding, the – the screams' – he paused, grimacing – 'all went. Silence and darkness. Until, out of nowhere – lord knows how – comes the sound of a bugle. And suddenly I'm back there in the middle of it all, as if it'd never stopped.'

A nudge from Florence, an expressive glance. Ante stared down at her hands and smiled.

Harry didn't notice. 'A hundred years,' he repeated, lifting his gaze back to Gil's. 'Unbelievable.'

'What I can't believe,' said Ante, 'is that you were in the army in the first place. If your – your accident in the loft happened four years before the First World War, and you were ten at the time – '

'The *first* – ?' broke in Gil. 'You're not telling me there've been more?'

'I'll explain later,' said Ante hurriedly. 'What I'm saying is, well, Harry, you can't be much more than seventeen now. Isn't that too young for the army?'

'I lied about my age. They didn't ask questions. It happened a lot.'

'You *lied* about your age? When you didn't need to be there at all?'

Harry gave a deep sigh. 'Look, Ante, I hadn't just killed my friend. I'd killed my brother. I didn't want to live anymore.'

Killed my friend. The words stabbed Ante's heart. Eyes fixed on her lap, she dug her hand into the ground, forcing earth under the fingernails. Beside her Florence sat silently, arms clasped round her knees, gazing at the river as if lost in thought.

At the river, that could heal wounds and wash away pain and yet not make everything right again.

Gil got up and stretched. 'I wonder where we are.' He walked a few paces up the slope and looked around. 'It feels a bit like Elysium but – oh!'

'What is it?' Florence rose to go after him.

'I think you'd better see this.'

There was an odd ring to his voice. Thrusting Harry's words to the back of her mind, Ante scrambled up to join them on the edge of a meadow dotted with wild flowers that rolled away to a shimmering blue sky. To the left, the ground sloped upwards in a series of little hills that seemed to curve round the rim of the vast canyon behind them. And to the right – her heart turned over. A great wave welled up inside her, so great she feared it would burst and sweep her away on a huge tide of – of what? Joy, certainly. And yet – and yet –

A green mountain rising high into the sky, its summit swathed in white cloud. A path winding up and up until it disappeared out of sight… in a flash she was sitting near the bank of another river, a greasy, sluggish, evil-smelling river, while beside her the strange, sandy-haired schoolboy with bare knees and scuffed lace-up shoes poured out his story. *And I knew, all the time, that I didn't belong here, that something was calling me…*

The green mountain. Gil's green mountain. He'd found it at last.

'Look!' Florence was at her shoulder. 'Those people – like before. The ones with the gold coins! At the jetty, remember?'

For this path wasn't empty. People moved along it in a line that snaked back down the mountain, over the river at its foot and away into the mist. Splashes glinted in the sun where the line met the water, here shallow enough to wade through.

'*Gold coins,*' murmured Ante, '*go round the Styx*. They must have circled the top of the canyon to get to this side – '

She broke off as Florence shouted, 'Hey, guys, wait for us!'

Gil and Harry were already striding across the meadow.

'Wait!' called Ante and made to follow.

She felt a hand on her shoulder.

'Ante, look.' Florence pointed at the ground just in front of them, then to where the boys walked several paces ahead.

'What's the matter? I can't see anything – oh.'

The rising sun warmed Ante's back and cast her shadow long in the grass before her. But where Gil and Harry walked there was no shadow.

Something clutched at her stomach. She looked at Florence and read the same uneasiness in her eyes. 'Gil, Harry! Where – where are you going?' she called out. 'What's the hurry?'

No reply. The space between them grew every moment. She sped up, breaking into a run, and at last drew near enough to the procession to see that it was composed, as before, of people of all ages and nationalities, all chatting and laughing together. No sign of the young men with baseball caps and clipboards. But where the path reached the foot of the mountain and began to wind upwards, another figure appeared.

An old man, older than anyone Ante had ever seen, stood to one side of the procession and regarded it with stern eyes. His long hair, white as snow, flowed over his shoulders and his beard reached down almost to his waist. The sun shone full on his face but his gaze never wavered on the people who, approaching him, fell silent before proceeding up the mountain.

'Halt.'

Reaching the boys, Ante and Florence stood before the old man whose brightness made them shield their eyes.

'You did not come with the others.'

'No,' said Gil. 'We came over the river. From down there.' He turned and pointed.

The people standing nearest to them gasped.

The old man looked at Gil. 'You crossed the river Lethe? Then you have been through Hades. Few are the souls that come that way. Ah!'

His eye had fallen on the golden bough in Ante's belt. Others in the crowd saw the brightness and drew back in wonder. But the old man betrayed no surprise. He remained silent for a moment before bringing his gaze to rest first on Harry, then on Gil. 'So,' he said. 'Your night was long but day has come at last.' Then, raising his bushy eyebrows, 'What are you waiting for? Have you not lost enough time already?'

Ante looked up, startled. But the old man wasn't looking at her or Florence. He seemed to have forgotten their existence completely.

Nor was he the only one.

A sense of foreboding seized Ante as Gil and Harry turned and fixed their gaze on the mountain, a strange look of longing in their eyes.

'*Gil*!' She reached out to grab his arm – and touched nothing.

Florence flung her arms around Harry, only to bring them back to her own body, empty.

'No,' sobbed Ante, 'No – please – Gil, Harry, don't go! Don't leave us – not now!'

'You can't!' cried Florence, trying again to embrace them, and again, and again.

It was no good. Tears filled Ante's eyes, brimming over and coursing down her cheeks.

Gil turned to look at her. In the sunlight his grey eyes shone like glass. 'We must,' he said. 'This is our path now. Not yours. If I could choose' – he dropped his gaze, reddening, before bringing it back to hers – 'I'd have no other friends, or travelling companions, or – or comrades in arms than you two. But you have your whole lives – ' he broke off and turned aside, blinking, as Harry put a hand on his shoulder.

Ante's arms filled with longing. If only she'd flung them round him while she still could! To feel his solid, broad shoulders under his scratchy flannel jacket, his thick sandy hair against her cheek…

'Promise me this,' said Gil, and his voice roughened, as if he was having trouble mastering it. 'Don't mess things up like me and Harry. I don't care' – glancing at Harry, he corrected himself – '*we* don't care how long it takes you to come after us, we'll be waiting. Somewhere up there. Goodbye, Ante. Goodbye Florence. Thanks for – for everything.'

'No.' Florence's voice came lower than a whisper. She barely breathed. 'No, no, no.'

'Goodbye, Florence. Goodbye Ante,' said Harry, the warmth in his brown eyes mingling with a kind of hunger. 'I wish I'd had the chance to get to know you properly. I'll make Gil tell me everything about you. But it won't be the same.'

'You're not going.' Florence shook her head. 'Not without us.'

Florence stared as Gil and Harry moved away, their light, almost transparent forms gliding towards the path. Then with the slightest of shifts, her gaze rested on the mountain beyond. A strange yearning gathered in her eyes.

Ante's heart stopped. 'No, Florence. We have to go back.' Every muscle in her body tensed. *Keep calm*, she told herself. *It doesn't mean anything. Florence has a shadow. She's not like them.*

No answer. No movement. Light outlined the fine profile, softening the far away expression on her face, flooding into her shadow…

The blue eyes flickered. Florence blinked as if waking from a dream. 'Wh – what happened?'

Ante let out a long breath. 'They're on their way,' she said. 'Look.'

Snatches of conversation floated back through the clear air as two sandy-haired figures, one tall and slight, the other shorter and stockier, joined the procession winding its way up the mountain.

'*I'm* the eldest now, you know.'

'No you're not. If I'm around 113, you're only 110.'

'Well, I'm bigger than you at any rate…'

The path turned a corner and they were gone.

CHAPTER THIRTY

The Return

'That's it, then,' sighed Florence.

Ante stared at the mountain. Its outline dissolved into smudges of green speckled with moving figures, fading into white cloud and blue sky. 'We didn't even say good-bye,' she croaked.

Florence turned on the old man who stood examining the slow stream of people as if nothing had happened. 'Why can't we go too?' she cried. 'We came through everything together. We *belong* together.'

'No. You do not belong together. They died a long time ago.'

'But…' Ante's voice trailed away. The years stretched out between her and the two boys, as dear to her as if they'd been her own brothers, born more than a century before.

'Then – what about us?' said Florence. 'Do we go back now?'

Without looking at her, the old man pointed towards the hills on their left. 'That way lies your path. Follow the bough. It will lead you whence you came.'

Ante gazed at the man's stern, bright profile and came to a sudden decision. *I've got to know. Know for certain. And if anyone can help, he can.* She summoned up her courage.

'Please Mr – Sir – ' she faltered as his eyes turned to hers. 'You seem to know all about us – '

'My name is Cato. My task is to guide people along the path that is right for them.'

'Then,' Ante pressed on, 'if we're to go back, does that – does that mean that we're both – we're both – '

Alive. Why couldn't she say it?

' – that everything will be all right?'

She held her breath. Beside her Florence stood still.

'I can only show you your path,' he said after a moment. 'I cannot show you its end.'

Ante sighed and turned to go.

But another thought struck her and she whisked round, speaking very fast. 'Mr Cato – please, can you tell me – did my – did my dad come this way? Tall man, lanky, quite young, looked a bit like me maybe. A while back, I mean. Nearly – '

'Six years ago. Yes, he came. I sent him on with the others.' There was a hint of softness in his expression.

A wave of joy rushed through Ante. 'Where is he? Can I see him?' But even as the words left her lips she knew the answer.

'One day. He is far up the mountain now.'

Joy. And pain. And longing. Her eyes strained to follow the path until it disappeared into cloud and distance; as if somehow she could pierce through and see beyond.

Then a hand put itself gently in hers. 'Come on, Ante,' whispered Florence.

They'd only gone a few paces when a call came from behind.

'Wait.' The line of people had come to a standstill as Cato shone the full beam of his face on them. 'You did well,' he said.

Only three words. But they felt good. Something to hold on to when everything and everyone she ever cared about seemed to slip from her grasp.

'Ante, are you all right?'

She could feel Florence's eyes fixed on her.

'I'm – I'm sorry about your dad.'

'It's OK.' She gulped. 'It's good, actually. At least now I – I know he's all right. I mean, I thought he would be, after what Penelope said, but still…I'm glad I know for sure.'

Florence nodded. A few steps later she said: 'Ante.'

'Yes?'

'You know that last Christmas at St Dunstan's, when you were Mary in the play – that was when your dad died, wasn't it? Mrs Jenkins was trying to make it up to you.'

'Yes.'

'I should've realised! If only she'd said that was why she gave you my part – '

'She did *what*?' Ante stood still.

'Didn't you know?' Florence's blue eyes widened. '*I* was meant to be Mary. I'd been practising, I'd learnt all the songs... then suddenly you were back at school again and it was *you*, not me, and I couldn't understand – you mean you didn't *know*?'

Ante stared at her, open-mouthed, her brain in a whirl. Memories flooded in: Mrs Jenkins bending down, her thin mouth set in a tight, anxious smile as she helped her into the deep blue robe and head dress, people in groups whispering and falling silent at her approach, her mother's eyes glowing above cheeks smudged with tears, the rickety wooden stage that smelt of dust and old paint – but as to how it all fitted together...

'I thought at first I must've done something wrong,' said Florence. 'But I knew I hadn't. So then all I could think was that you – you – '

'Stole it! *That's* what it was!'

Florence nodded. 'I'd been telling my mum and dad and gran for weeks. They came to watch and there I was, not Mary at all, just some stupid angel! That's when I decided, no matter what, I was never going back to St Dunstan's. And then, years later, you turn up at Northwell and straight away get picked to play the Remembrance Day solo; it was like, here we go again.'

'*That's* why you hated me so much,' murmured Ante. 'I never did understand.'

'It all seems so stupid now,' sighed Florence as they set off again. 'And such a waste. We could've been friends.'

Could have? A chill ran down Ante's spine. The hillside drew closer. Thickening vegetation lined the path, hemming it in. Time was running out.

She tried to keep the tremor out of her voice. 'Well, we can now, can't we?'

The path was becoming stony. A black shape loomed ahead, framed by a jagged edge of rock. They plunged into the tunnel, drawn upwards on some invisible current.

And Florence hadn't replied! In the dim light Ante couldn't make out her expression. Battling against the force driving her on, she tore the bough from her belt and held it up.

'*Florence!*'

The pale cheeks were wet with tears. 'I'm scared, Ante. I – I don't know what we're going to find. I feel – strange.'

Was it the poor light – or did her figure seem even slighter than before – shadowy even?

'No!' cried Ante. 'We're going to be all right! We're *both* – '

'So I want to say, thanks. For – for being the best friend I ever had. In case I don't make – in case I can't say it again.'

'*What are you talking about?*' Ante's throat felt tight. 'You're – going to be – fine.'

Blank rock straight ahead. Slow down, they must *slow down*. But her feet no longer touched the ground.

'Take my hand!' she yelled suddenly.

'What?'

'Take it!'

An ear-splitting crack. The bough flew from Ante's grasp. Something wrenched her other arm forward and she fell heavily. Boards swayed beneath her. Clouds of dust filled the air and stung her eyes and for a moment she lay coughing and gasping, aware of nothing but the weight pulling at the end of her arm and the grip of fingers round her own.

'Hold on!' Dust clogged her throat. She could hardly speak. 'Someone will come!'

The cloud settled. Straight ahead, where balustrades and hand rail should turn the corner of the organ loft, splinters of wooden uprights framed a gap in which Florence's face showed pale above the floorboards, lips parted, eyes frozen with fear. With one hand she held on to Ante with all her might. With the other she clutched at a broken balustrade, trying to pull her body back up over the edge, on to the balcony floor –

SNAP.

'No!' screamed Ante. Her arm jerked painfully as the rotten balustrade sheered off altogether, plunging Florence's whole body to hang over nothingness, held only by Ante's hand clutching hers.

CHAPTER THIRTY-ONE

Remembrance

Ante's arm stretched and stretched, sweat pouring down her sleeve, smaller fingers sliding though hers – *no, don't let them, don't let go* – the crash of a door underneath and Florence's hand slipping, she couldn't hold on, she was losing her – then the sudden, sickening lightening of the weight on her arm followed instantly by a thud down below, her wail of despair rising over the voices crying out beneath her…

Voices. Two voices. Florence's scream mingled with a man bellowing, 'Good god, girl, what – ' ending in a gasp and a thud.

'Florence!' cried Ante. She didn't dare move to look over. '*Florence!*'

The blood was beating so hard in her head she could hear nothing but a great rushing noise, and the sound of her own deep gasping for air. Footsteps came running through the door below and clattered up the stairs on the other side of the wall behind her, together with voices, cries of alarm – *quiet!* Her mind screamed, *be quiet! I've got to hear her, got to hear if she's all right –*

236

Down below a creaking of floorboards, shoes scraping and stumbling over broken pieces of timber, the sound of someone – no, more than one person – groaning and getting to their feet, and through it all the voice Ante wanted to hear more than anything else in the world, faint, shaky but unmistakeable.

'Ante, I'm – I'm OK. But Mr Randall's hurt. I'm really sorry, Mr Randall. If you hadn't been there to break my fall – '

A rasping sound cut off her words; the dry gasping for breath of someone who's just had the wind knocked out of them.

Then, painfully: 'If I – hadn't been – here – and if – this floor was still – flagstones, not timber – you'd have – broken a leg, young lady. If not two. Do you know, about a hundred years ago, there *was* some poor boy who…'

Ante laid her face on the floor of the organ loft and gave herself up to waves of tears and laughter.

Agreeing to meet the Head of Music in the assembly hall before afternoon school had been the best decision of her life.

★ ★ ★

'Ante, there's something I want to – ouch. Watch it.'

'Sorry.' Skirting the bandaged right arm, Ante fell in on Florence's left as she walked across the playground towards the games field. 'How's the sprain?'

'Getting better. Yours?'

'No orchestra for me this week. After that it should be OK. Not sure who'll be conducting it though – poor Mr Randall, I bet he wishes he'd never walked in just then.'

'Well I don't,' said Florence. 'And he said himself, it could've been so much worse than a few bruised ribs and a fractured wrist. Now come on, we've got to hurry or lunch break will be over.'

Mud squelched under Ante's feet as they crossed the football pitch. Tree branches waved in the wind, tossing leaves into the white sky. On the far side, where the ground sloped down to the river, stood the tall stone cross, a dull splash of crimson at its foot all that remained of the ceremony a few days before. Drawing near, Florence leaned down and pulled the wreath of poppies to one side.

Four panels made up the base. As Florence bent back the wet grasses obscuring the lettering, Ante began to read, her voice shrinking to a whisper. 'The Great War, 1914 to 1918. In memory of those who gave their lives – '

She couldn't go on. Her throat felt raw. On the back of her head and neck the hairs stood on end.

Florence's fingers brushed down the names carved into the panel, resting on one about half-way down. A lot of names, twelve at least; how could there be so many when the school had been so small? They dissolved into a blur of grey stone and Florence's hand, red with cold; but not before she'd read the one she knew would be there.

'It's Harry,' said Florence, 'See? *Henry Marow.* It's him.'

Ante nodded, unable to speak. So where was... her eyes darted to the panel next to it and she bent to snatch the grass away. He must be there too, somewhere. With his funny, weird first name in full, like Harry's. Not shortened to the one she knew best.

Except that... she sat back on her heels.

Florence broke into her thoughts. 'He's not there, remember? Gil died before it happened.'

Her arms fell to her sides. Tears swelled her throat. Nothing for Gil then, not even a name on a piece of stone. Only a fragment of school history, half-forgotten, and their own memories of a boy in strange, old-fashioned uniform, with bare knees and socks round his ankles, sunlight flooding his eyes as he turned to smile at them one last time.

She wiped her hands on her skirt and got to her feet. 'We'd better get back.'

People bobbed across the playground ahead of them. Ante tried to imagine the school as it would have been in Gil's day when only the main school building existed. She pictured him waking up in a dormitory somewhere above the science labs, hurrying downstairs to the dark, panelled lobby and the assembly hall where Dr Northwell waited, hymn book in hand...

The lobby. The panelled walls. Ante stopped. 'I know where to find him,' she said.

'But we'll be late!' said Florence.

Never mind. She had to do this now. Bearing left towards the main school building, she pushed her way up the steps through a stream of Year Sixes in football kit pouring out of the door.

'Not back to the organ loft,' pleaded Florence. 'They'll kill us if they find us there again. You know what the Head said.'

'Not the organ loft.'

She turned left towards the assembly hall. There, on either side of the door, school photographs lined the walls: seas of blue and grey uniform and sun-dazzled stares. Then,

'*Yes.*'

A brown, faded photograph, its mount mottled with age. In front of an ivy-covered wall sat a craggy-faced gentleman with long whiskers, wearing a black gown over his suit and waistcoat, both hands resting on top of a stick. On one side of him a formidable-looking woman in a thick, black, ankle-length dress; on the other, a couple of young men in high white collars, their dark suits set off by watch chains looped into waistcoat pockets.

But it wasn't the staff of Northwell School photographed a hundred years ago that mattered. Ranged around their teachers were a number of boys, eldest at the back, youngest sitting cross-legged on the grass in front. Some of the littler ones wore sailor suits; the taller ones, thick flannel jackets over high-necked shirts and shorts to their knees, a style of uniform at once alien and terribly, endearingly familiar. Looking at this long-lost group of boys in their stiff clothes, Ante could feel the roughness of the material on her skin and how the high collars chafed in hot weather.

'*There.*'

A stockily-built boy with thick, tousled hair stood at a slight angle, his light-grey eyes gazing calmly out of the picture, his face somehow wearing a cheerful expression, even though he wasn't smiling. The faded sepia couldn't bring out the freckles, yet Ante and Florence knew they were there: pale sprinklings on Gil's skin that matched the sandy-red of his hair.

'1909,' whispered Florence. 'The year before Harry arrived.'

Ante shivered. 'Poor Gil. He had no idea what was coming.'

'None of them did.'

Heat prickled Ante's eyes. She blinked. Stone, ivy, grass, pale figures in grey flannel and sailor suits, all dissolved in a haze of brown and faded white.

'Come on,' said Florence in her ear. 'The bell went ages ago.'

One last look. Then arm in arm with Florence, she made for the door.